# THE FORT

## *Also by Storm Jameson*

# THE FORT

By

STORM JAMESON

CASSELL
*and Company Limited*
London, Toronto, Melbourne
and Sydney

01446946

*First published 1941*

610

ACCRINGTON

Printed in Great Britain by T. and A. Constable Ltd.
at the University Press, Edinburgh
F.941

*For*

HERMON OULD

*with the writer's respect and affection*

# CHAPTER I

## I

THE cellars of this farm in north-eastern France were the oldest part of the house, since in 1919 they had only needed to be cleared of rubbish, and there they were, almost intact. An admirable foundation for the new house which, so far as looks go, had nothing to commend it. What raw bricks and glass could rebuild was rebuilt, and the model in mother-of-pearl of the Clock-Tower at Evreux, snatched up despairingly in 1914, was given back to a room in which everything else was new, cold, unable to say anything. The son of the house was missing—since 1914— and with him every memory of him. This included the lines drawn on the door of the kitchen, marking his growth. Mme Broussard, his mother, dying six weeks after she came to live in the new house, could find nothing to take with her in her last glance; nothing was familiar, wallpaper, cupboard, quilt; even the staircase creaked in a new place. She was not able to see through the small window fields unnaturally wrinkled, still stiff with anguish—the soil had been cleared of everything except a single root, a fibre, of France, poor, hard—and the Ancre, a dozen fields away but visible as it had never been visible from a window in her house, because the line of poplars had disappeared, rubbed out, not one, not one, left. Mme Broussard died in giving birth to a daughter, and though no doubt she was foolish to have a second child more than twenty years after the other, she had at least not been foolish enough to think, as her husband did—for how long? a minute?—that a time which has been lost can be found again by the loser, and that one place is as good as another.

To return to the cellars of the farm. There were three of them, opening into each other by wide gaps in the thick walls. The middle cellar could be made habitable. Air and a little light reached it from the yard, through a wide shaft in the back wall. Sloping wooden shutters in the yard covered the mouth of this shaft. Nothing much was stored in this cellar now: a set of old harness hung from a nail, together with a coil of thin rope; along one wall a stone shelf was empty except—it would have been surprising in any year but this—for various objects belonging to a present-day soldier's kit. Against the opposite wall a rolled-up blanket, and at the same side of the room a bench long enough for a man to lie down. A rough kitchen table stood close against the shaft, as close as possible to the light. There were two nondescript chairs.

In the cellar to the right a half-dozen stone stairs led up to the kitchen of the farm, through a hatch in the floor. Even when this was open, so little light came through that the stairs were only roughly visible to a man standing in the middle cellar. He could see them clearly if someone came down carrying a light.

It was evening, June 13, 1940.

The shutters that let light into the middle cellar were closed. It was lit by a candle and a lamp, a common brass lamp, of the sort you buy in a village shop. There were two men, infantry officers, in the cellar. One, an Englishman, was reading at the table, his book held in the circle of light. The other, the Frenchman, watched him, idly, sunk in his own thought, his shoulders a little drawn up, as though he were standing in the rain. Both were middle-aged; both, as their tunics made plain, had served in the last war. A pair of oddly-shaped crutches were propped against the table. They belonged to the Englishman, Major Ward.

The hatch at the top of the stairs was lifted. Louis Broussard, the farmer, came down the stairs, stiffly, a man who carried his land on the soles of his feet. The French officer, Captain Redon, turned to him as he came in.

'Well, what's the news?'

'Evening, Broussard,' Ward said. 'Can't you open the shutters for a moment? It's unbearable in here.'

'One fine night a German will poke his beak down the shaft,' Broussard grumbled. 'That my God will be the end of us.' He walked back to the foot of the stairs, and shouted. 'Martine. Martine. Open the cellar. Quick. This Englishman is stifling.'

'Thanks, I was,' Ward said.

Someone, Martine, lifted back the heavy wooden flaps. Air and light, the clear light without languid after-thoughts, of northern France, came into the cellar. The Englishman stretched his hand out and turned down the lamp on the table.

'The crutches are all right?' Broussard asked.

'Excellent. I'm much obliged to you. You did a grand job. Another fortnight, a shirt and a pair of trousers, and I'll push on them to the coast.'

'And then?'

'I shall have an excellent meal before taking the afternoon boat—onion soup, sole, chicken fried in cream. A slice of Brie. A rather young claret. No coffee. French coffee is undrinkable.'

'I asked you if you had news,' Captain Redon said.

Ward looked at him. 'Unless he spends his days in an attic window, counting heads, German heads, on the Albert road, he hasn't. Where could he get news? The Boches are between us and news. The last time I saw a French plane, five days ago, it had its back to us.'

'You have seen English planes?' Redon said gently.

'I have some news,' Broussard said. 'A relation of mine—a nephew of my mother's first cousin, to be exact—has turned up. He lives—he lived—in Beaucourt. He has just paid for his own shop, and he stayed until he saw the first German tank working its snout into the street, then bolted as far as Soissons. Then doubled back. He hasn't been home, he dropped in here to ask if I knew what had become of his shop. Me! As if I had time to get myself arrested running into the town to protect his rolls of cloth. They're making night-shirts for Goering of your cloth now, I said to him. He's upstairs, blubbering a little.'

'I'll talk to him,' Redon said.

Turning his head, with the air of a bull watching a man cross his field, Broussard watched him up the stairs.

'Where are the other two?' he asked Ward.

Ward nodded towards the completely dark cellar on the other side. 'Asleep. They don't argue when they're sleeping.'

'There are too many people in these cellars now,' Broussard said drily.

'Sorry. I've been here how long?'

'Eight days. When they brought you, your friends said they would send a car or an ambulance in a few hours.'

'The Germans move too quickly nowadays. They don't seem to know what is expected of them.'

'They are still my God moving,' Broussard said. 'Not tanks now, but men and more men. From the long field—that is, two and a quarter miles in a straight line from the Amiens road—I can see a cloud of dust coming from Bapaume and going towards Amiens. It advances at the rate of three miles an hour. Is that the German walking speed? They must waddle like ducks.'

'Why didn't you clear out?' Ward asked.

'I was in the last war. I had no choice. I'm too old this time. How old would you say I was?'

'Fifty-five.'

'Sixty-nine,' Broussard said. 'We keep our fresh colour in my family. I have my teeth. Other things as well. But I'm too old to turn off my land except with a rifle in my backside. It's mine. There were Broussards here with the Spaniards. You can believe me. I don't say it's the best soil in France. All I say is it suits me. In 1918, after the Armistice, my cousin's widow—he was killed off at Verdun, poor sinner—offered me his farm on the Sèvre, on easy terms. She was a weak creature. I went there to look at it. Do you know that part of the country? What trees, my God! What grass! Hedges as high as a barn, water everywhere—you could open your mouth and drink the soil. Wherever you turned, trees, hills. I told Widow Coulon I'd take her farm off her. Then I came up here, to look at the place. Nothing here, not a sign of the house except the cellars, mud, mud-holes, you could count on a fine crop of barbed wire and rags for next year. As though I'd been struck I thought: Why, I can see for miles. It was a fact—you know yourself, this country is as flat as a blow. On my cousin's land I was always running my eye into something, a hill or a forest. It would have finished me. I stayed here. It's a fact my wife never liked the house. She grumbled. It was colder than the other. She used to see a line of poplars from the bedroom, now she could see the river. She missed our son—he was killed—she missed chiefly the door of the old kitchen. Every June fifth she used to put a mark there for the top of his head. She died six weeks after we came back. No doubt I was a fool to start another child more than twenty years after the first. I thought we should begin again. One house is as good as another—why not one child and one day? It seems it's not the same for women as for land.'

'I'm surprised you haven't sent your daughter away,' Ward said.

'Send her where? She's safer here than running about the roads.'

'That's true. Those poor devils near Arras had thrown away everything—even the hope of reaching the next village alive. The German pilots were coming down low enough to machine-gun them in the ditches. Like pouring boiling water on ants. They sprawled there in the sun afterwards. . . . I saw a child move an arm in a heap of women and rags, but by the time I reached her she had died. Her mouth—it was wide open—was full of the bread she had been eating.'

'Always the same Boche,' Broussard said. 'When they were killing each other we used to say: After all, they're stupid. But as soon as they get here they're Boches.'

'What would you do with them?' Ward asked.

'Kill them.'

'You can't kill a nation.'

'You asked me what I would do if I could. If we'd been sensible in 1918 we'd have killed everything male in Germany. Every son and every husband, and every clerk, farmer, postman. Especially the farmers.'

'You would have been ashamed afterwards,' Ward said.

'I'd risk that. Think of waking one morning, everything clear, simple, the sky a fine French grey, the wind smelling of France, only of France, not a tree that would have a German axe to it that day—nor any day. Every step you take is on roads no German will put his foot on again, there are no German rivers, only French ones, and any word anyone speaks means what it has always meant, nothing more, nothing less. 'Think of it.'

'And at night,' Ward said, 'you would be leaning all your weight against doors and windows to keep out the German silence.'

'It won't happen. They'll be allowed to live.' Broussard moved towards the stairs. 'You're comfortable?'

'I've been here before,' Ward said quickly. 'Yesterday I hobbled to the end of that cellar. I hadn't noticed how far it runs. I recognised it suddenly. I spent a night here in October 1916.'

'I hope you were comfortable.'

'I was cold.'

'Alone? You were alone?'

'There were two of us,' Ward said.

'Did your friend come back this year?'

'He was killed next day, in one of your fields,' Ward said. 'There was a trench in front of the cellars, it went through the field and turned left over the road . . .'

Broussard interrupted him. 'I know, I know, I filled it in. You can see it if you step back a few yards.'

As he reached the foot of the stairs, Captain Redon began coming down. Broussard waited.

'Did you get any sense out of him?' he asked.

'A little.'

'You were lucky. He's an idiot. . . . Is there anything you want before you go? You're leaving tonight?'

'Nothing,' Redon said. 'Thanks. We leave at half-past ten.'

'You have a fine night,' Broussard said. 'The sixty-eighth perfectly clear night since the middle of April. Warm.' He put his foot on a stair, hesitated, turned round. 'Good luck, sir.'

Without hoping for any answer, he went off.


2


'What did you hear?' Ward asked.

'I can tell you what I think is happening,' Redon said. 'This fellow left Soissons on the night of the eleventh, when the German tanks got there. He's like the others. Instead of hiding in their cellars they bolt into the streets, into the fields. You've seen rabbits rush in front of your car at night? He ran away. . . . Soissons has been besieged oftener than any town in France, and the stones talk—before he left he heard they were in Rheims.'

'Well?'

'They may have reached the Marne. . . . They'll be held there.'

'It's possible,' Ward said.

'Anything else is impossible.'

'Two months ago you would have told me it was impossible for France to be invaded.'

'I? No. Never,' Redon said, with energy. 'I knew better. We were fools to sit waiting for them. We should have taken every tank we had in our hands and invaded Germany. Last year. A month ago. Last week! In three days we should have been in Munich. We should have exchanged cities. German tanks in Paris! What of it? Ours are in Berlin. It's true we have fewer tanks. . . . But German civilians would have been as terrified as our shopkeepers and clerks. More terrified, because they've been told to think with their blood. The sight of one of our tanks would have frozen it.'

'Not a bad idea,' Ward said. 'Merely impossible. You could bring it off if both countries were ready to panic and the generals on both sides had imagination and energy. But everyone knows that the imagination and the energy are all on one side. In any war! How else can you start a war?'

'Do you think German shopkeepers would have laughed at tanks?'

18

'Oh, don't think I admire the Germans,' Ward said. 'They have certain virtues, but they're servile.'

'They boast. They wanted this war.'

'You're wrong. We could have had peace if we'd fed them after the last war, and flattered instead of scolding and humiliating them. I saw respectable German women in Essen—how ugly they were after the last war, poor creatures—forced to stand in the gutter while French soldiers walked past them.'

'Pitying your enemies is an English tic,' Redon said calmly. 'Like laughing loudly in the street. Besides—it's stupid to talk to us about peace with the Germans. Oh, you can talk, you can turn rich tourists out of their hotels for conferences, you can be photographed shaking hands and signing a treaty. And behind everything—everybody in both countries sees it, the taximen, schoolmasters, prostitutes—you have the same nail waiting to be trodden on. They're many and greedy. We are rich and few.'

'Nonsense.'

'You don't like to admit it. It makes you uncomfortable.'

'My dear fellow,' Ward said, 'why should you quarrel with the Germans? Bordeaux

wines are better than hock. The Rhône is a
finer river than the Rhine. More civilised.
Lighter. Your forests give off more sun than
the Black Forest with its pines and absurd nudist
camps. No one in his senses prefers storks to
magpies. The balance is actually on your side.
You were afraid of each other. This war was quite
unnecessary and you took care it should be inevit-
able. You make me tired, the two of you.'

'Very well, we were afraid,' Redon said. 'A
war isn't a practical joke.'

'No, it's a mistake.'

'Wrong, you're wrong,' Redon exclaimed.
'You think wars don't happen on purpose?
What nonsense! They happen when a com-
mander-in-chief orders his army to cross the
frontier of another country. It's perfectly simple.
He can see that it's a frontier. There is a customs
officer, a sentry. The air on the other side is
different. The quality of the light changes
when you cross. It weighs lighter or heavier.
Never mind, they step over and have to be driven
back, with loss and anguish. What could be
simpler? Or viler?'

'A road near Arras was looking vile enough
when I saw it,' Ward said. 'The German tanks had
run over their own wounded and some children.'

'An accident of this war. War is bad enough without accidents. . . . I was in the line near Sedan in May. One of my companies had a boy of eighteen from the Vendée. I know those Vendéens, they complain, they curse—at the beginning of a long march they walk as though the next step were their last—and at the end of the march they begin singing and smiling. Where was I? This boy. During the attack he was in the line for three days without being able to sleep. The third night he fell asleep in the observation post. It was the colonel who found him there. He was shot.'

'Couldn't you save him?' Ward asked.

'I didn't try.'

'A very hard case.'

'It was wretched. And necessary. I can see the boy. He had a smooth childish forehead and a friendly smile.'

'The French colonel on our right,' Ward said, 'took his battalion out of the line without orders—and without a word to us. He did more damage than your sentry, we were caught and had to fight our way out.'

'Either he lost his nerve, or—he will probably be shot.'

'He didn't lose his nerve.'

21

'France is torn in two,' Redon said. 'And in the middle of a war.'

'And you? What do you think?'

'I have no views,' Redon said. 'We must save France.'

'Oh, quite, quite. . . . Do your two young men think so?'

'I find it difficult to talk to them—even though one of them is my nephew.'

'Vidal?' Ward asked.

'Yes. Lucien Vidal. My sister's boy. His father was killed at the end of the last war. He was very intelligent, very brave.'

'This young man hasn't had much chance to be brave,' Ward said.

'My God, these things are not chance.'


3

Second-lieutenant Pierre Masson came in from the darkness of the cellar on the left. He came in with an air of formality, and saluted Redon.

'Can I speak to you, sir?'

'What?'

'I should like to start now,' Masson said.

'What do you mean?' Redon said sharply.

'Alone, sir.'

'Why?'

Masson dropped his air of respect for a senior officer, and spoke in a gentle voice with his usual freedom and mockery.

'I like being alone. It saves my temper.'

'Do you expect me to be interested in your likings?' Redon said.

'If I were one of two junior officers under your orders, no,' Masson said. 'But your authority is worth less all the time. You can't stop certain people from wanting us to be defeated, and you can't order me to risk my life with them.'

'You're talking about Mr Vidal,' Redon said.

'About your nephew.'

'You're both under my orders,' Redon said. 'You'll be punished if you refuse an order. There's no other relationship.'

'We can't live like rats,' said Ward, 'and keep up the Guards touch, you know. I should let him talk.'

'Thanks for the rats,' Masson said.

'If anything he has to say has any relevance . . .' Redon said.

'Is it relevant to say that Mr Vidal talks treason?' Masson said.

'Explain that,' Redon said.

'Rotten sentimental treason about France bleeding from a million wounds. And about the virtues of the Germans.'

'Heavens, is that all?' Ward said.

'You have to live with the English to know how frivolous they are,' Masson said. 'It would be unbelievable.'

'This Englishman is amusing himself with you,' Redon said quietly. 'You've said enough.'

He turned his back, and after a moment Masson walked to the back of the shelter and stood looking up the shaft.

'Where are you going to make for?' Ward asked.

'The Marne obviously. Headquarters will be at Châlons.'

'You think so?'

'What d'you mean?' Redon said.

'Your troops weren't able to hold a prepared line, on the Canal and the lower Somme,' Ward said carefully. 'Why should you believe they're holding the Marne?'

'I should know if the Marne had been lost.'

'A bad sign. You're turning mystical,' Ward said.

'Not at all. We're in a part of the country where again and again the ground has had to give

24

cover to human kindness and liberty. All its rivers run through this living chalk. If the Germans have crossed one of them the news will be repeated from field to field in an hour.'

'I'm a foreigner, I shouldn't hear it,' Ward said.

'Well?'

'My belief is that the weight of this second defeat will throw them back as far as the Seine.'

Masson turned round. 'He means that when the French start to run they run farther and faster than the English.'

'Once he gives way any soldier runs as far and as quickly as he can, until he's stopped,' Ward said.

'Exactly,' Redon said curtly. 'Ours will be stopped on the Marne.'

Second-lieutenant Lucien Vidal came in unobtrusively from the cellar on the left, and stood listening. His right wrist was bandaged, and in a sling made from two handkerchiefs.

'It's more reasonable to expect them to hold a line from Rouen to Troyes, through Paris,' Ward said.

'Without help,' Masson said gently.

Ward looked at him. 'Why without help? Obviously English troops will be landed—at some point between Havre and Nantes.'

25

'And you dislike mysticism,' Masson said. 'The training of every French staff officer should include a course on holding a line until the English get there.'

'Be quiet,' Redon said sharply.

'Let him talk,' Ward said, smiling. 'Besides, he's right.'

'That has nothing to do with it,' Redon said.

'How like my father you are,' Masson smiled. 'He's been telling me for years to shut up and leave politics alone. I would if he could be trusted. But he only worries about his cabbages. And his liver.'

Vidal turned on him. 'He knew we should fight for his cabbages.'

'Not at all. He was always talking about peace. He wanted a pact with Hitler, quickly. You would like him.'

'This charming talk in front of an ally,' Captain Redon said.

Ward laughed. 'My dear fellow, have you ever been at a military council between allies? One of them compliments the other on his bold policy, and knowing he is being accused of rashness, the other says: Your troops are magnificent, they'll stand anything. He means: You've killed fewer than I expected from the incompetence of your staff. They smile, they listen politely or blankly. They're careful, loyal, decent. Then they salute each other, one left standing, smiling and innocent, on the steps of a comfortable château, the other stepping into his car, and both of them turn quickly to a subordinate and say: But my God, what an ass.'

'Is that what you think about us, sir?' Masson said.

'That's enough,' Redon said. He turned to Vidal. 'Your wrist?'

'Painful,' Vidal said, 'but it's all right.'

'Pity it's your right,' Ward said.

'Oh, I'm left-handed,' Vidal said easily.

'We leave in half an hour,' Redon said to him. 'As soon as we reach Châlons you can report and then find your regiment. Your wrist can wait.'

'I want to get back,' Vidal said.

'Of course . . . A retreat is demoralising.'

'I'm not demoralised.'

'Why should you be? But a soldier, especially a young soldier, loses his grip when he loses touch with the enemy. Too many ordinary things get between them. If you have to kill a man it's a pity to let your idea of him become confused by fields and peaceful nights.'

'I was in touch, as you call it, with the enemy

near Strasbourg,' Vidal said drily. 'I used to see a German, a young man, washing himself every day, in full view of our post, on the other side of the Rhine. He was tall and dark, and he had a way of stretching his arms and yawning that reminded me—I don't know what—of every fine morning of my life. I didn't hate him.'

'You needn't. You can leave that to politicians.'

'I find it perfectly easy to hate Germans,' Masson said pointedly. 'I hate the pleasure they get out of lying to themselves. I hate their habit of doubling everything, hills, lakes, trees, with a myth that swells them to twice their proper size. I hate their cruelty above all, and their wretched pity for themselves. They were meant to be simple and dignified—look at their large women! Then some ass borrowed the idea of a superman and since then they've only been ridiculous and detestable; and yet they ask to be loved and they dream they're killing the grown-ups who haven't admired them. It's our bad luck to live next door to these murderous sleep-walkers.'

'You even talk like a politician,' Redon said. He turned to Ward. 'Can I borrow your map for an hour.'

'Certainly.'

Redon took a second candle, stuck in a saucer,

from the shelf, lit it, and withdrew into the cellar on the right. The weak light of the candle passed across the steps. He could be heard dragging a chair or a box to the far side of the cellar.


### 4

The cellar had become almost dark, though it was still half light in the yard.

'I must have a light,' Ward said. 'See to the shutters, one of you.'

'I'll go up,' Vidal said.

Masson had gone back to the foot of the shaft.

'You needn't,' he said carelessly, 'the girl is still out there.' He raised his voice. 'Martine.'

They heard a girl's thin voice. 'Yes?'

'Will you drop the shutters?'

'Yes.'

'Do you want help?' Masson asked.

'No.'

Lucien Vidal had kept his eyes on the other young man's face during this brief talk. He turned away when the shutters were folded down. Major Ward had been lighting the lamp on the table. Opening his book again, he began to read. He sat with his back to the shaft, so that he had only to look up to take in the whole room, and the two young men. Pierre Masson moved towards the stairs. Vidal spoke, with an impulsive gesture towards him, and he stood still to listen.

'Need we go on quarrelling?'

'No. The arguments are very stale,' Masson said.

'They're clumsy. I don't reach you with mine.'

'Because we're not face to face, not proper enemies. We grew up with the same fear and guilt, they weren't even ours, they were given us with our first toy. My father felt as ashamed of surviving the war as though he'd only managed it by deserting his friends who were killed. And he expected the Germans to invade again, looking for him. He's a farmer, a poor farmer, he had only to turn the soil in his own fields to feel that they were as afraid as he was.'

'Where was your farm?' Vidal asked.

'On the frontier, near Charleville. A cold rather deep stream ran along the edge of it to the Meuse. If I never see it again, the stream is the only thing I shall regret. That and the paper boats I used to launch on it, with my fingers frozen. We were abominably poor. I remember being ill, I was a child, I had caught fever, and my sister comforted me by stroking my head with her long fingers and looked in it for lice at the same time. It was very soothing.'

'I've never been poor,' Vidal said.

'We weren't the only ones who were afraid. The rich feared us and distrusted us. What were we up to when we sat and talked for an hour on the bench of some wretched café? And then both our fears were confronted by Hitler, but where my father instinctively hated him, yours——'

'My father was killed,' Vidal said.

'His brothers were not,' Masson said quickly. 'They make speeches praising Germany, they envy the Nazis because disobedient and dissatisfied Germans have been silenced, you can even walk past a concentration camp and hear nothing, not a word, not a single scream. Yes, and they're horribly afraid of this obedient nation with its energy and its millions of steel tanks. All our arguments come down to this: I fear and hate the Nazis, you fear me and you admire them because they've found ways of killing me, in Dachau, in Madrid. Thousands of deaths.'

'You wanted to add the deaths of thousands of French people,' Vidal said.

'That's what you said when we wanted to crush Hitler.'

'You wanted war.'

'We wanted to crush him in time. He was weak at the beginning.'

'It meant another war,' Vidal said harshly. 'Call it what you like.'

'Aren't we at war?'

'Thanks to you.'

'Tell me,' Masson said quietly. 'What would you do now? Surrender?'

'No. Make terms.'

'Terms! With people without conscience or heart! We couldn't make ourselves understood. What do you suppose a Nazi understands by the words for honesty or mercy or pity?'

'Will it be easier when they've destroyed Chartres?'

'It would never be easy,' Masson said. 'Our country with its shabby villages round a Romanesque church, its workmen who are artists and its artists who are really peasants, its different minds, voices, arms, is facing a Germany which is one factory, one voice, one man, it has silenced all its voices except one that Goethe wouldn't have understood, it denies its past, it denies freedom, idleness, gentleness. How can a country with as many words for freedom as it has hands kneading bread and tongues clacking

32

away in the streets, how can it make terms with this senseless giant? Tell me.'

'If we don't, France is done for.'

'You talk as though France were only so many towns and provinces, and so many little clerks, husbands, market-gardeners, young men like us, whose existences will be left to us after surrender, as after defeat. But what about the other France? What about Rabelais and Voltaire and Stendhal and Charles Péguy? What about the promises we made to other nations, to keep them up to the mark in freedom, in wine, in living? Do you want to hear the excuses they will make for us?'

Major Ward had stopped reading when Masson raised his voice. He sat and watched, half amused, half uneasy.

'The man who stops this war won't need your excuses,' Vidal exclaimed.

'It won't be stopped.'

'Wait.'

'You're very windy, aren't you,' Masson said.

Vidal turned pale. 'You come to Paris from your village and run about gaping at the Seine, and the boulevards and the Louvre. You haven't the wit to see the rottenness, and the Jew squatting everywhere.'

'What's all this about?' Major Ward said.

Masson turned on him. 'Something you can't understand—unless you have defeatists in England.'

Captain Redon came into the cellar. He stood just inside the doorway, and neither young man noticed him.

'It wouldn't matter to you,' Vidal said vehemently, 'that Chartres was a pile of dust and every other child dead so long as your friends could creep out of their cellars afterwards. You and your lice.'

Redon spoke to Vidal. 'Go and wait in there.' He stretched his arm back towards the cellar he had just left, and turned to Masson. 'I'm going out to look round. You'll come with me. . . . Neither of you can be trusted to behave properly.'

He and Masson went up the stairs, and Lucien Vidal went quickly to the other cellar.


5

For a moment Major Ward sat on alone, his book open, but not reading. The noise of footsteps and voices started up suddenly in the room over the cellar to the right. The hatch at the top of the stairs was flung open. Broussard came down. He walked clumsily sideways, because he was holding a candle for an English soldier, a young second-lieutenant. The young man hesitated when he reached the foot of the stairs, and walked a little unsteadily into the middle cellar. Lucien Vidal appeared, excited and interested, and stood in the doorway.

'I found him crossing the low field,' Broussard said. 'He was half asleep.'

'I've been out for some days, sir,' the young man said apologetically to Ward.

'Thanks, Broussard,' Ward said. 'You're a good scout.'

'You find anything my God in the fields nowadays,' Broussard said.

He went away, looking inquisitively at Vidal as he pushed past.

'Sit down,' Ward said. 'Name.'

'Murray.'

'What d'you say?' Ward exclaimed. 'Where d'you come from?'

'My company was in the line near Cambrai——'

Ward interrupted him. 'No, no, England.'

'Stockbridge, sir. Hampshire.'

'There's a good trout river,' Ward said. 'I've fished it.'

35

'Richard Murray?' Lucien Vidal said suddenly.

Both Englishmen ignored him. He had taken a step forward, and now drew back.

'Well, what happened?' Ward said.

'My company was cut off on June the fifth. We found suddenly we had the Boches behind us and on both sides. Captain Smith decided we would hold on and try to fall back at night. We didn't know what was happening or how many Germans we had behind us. During the day we held off two attacks, then at ten-thirty, when we began moving, we were shelled for half an hour, Smith and the other officer were killed, we couldn't do anything, I had a dozen men with me, we found some sort of cover and next day we lay out. Just before dark a sergeant turned up from another company, I haven't fathomed it yet, there were others besides us in the mess. He crawled from one man to the next telling us which way to try to go on our own— he was a splendid fellow——'

'What was his name?'

'Griffith. A Welshman.'

'Thin and sallow, a long bony nose, and a brown eye, coming at you like a gimlet.'

'You know him?' Murray said.

'Oh, yes, he was at Crécy. Go on.'

'I and a corporal stayed together. He'd been hit in the arm. We lay up in daylight, of course, and moved at night. He was a Cockney, a proper young wharf rat. His wound began to go wrong, he was too bad to move, and we stayed two days and nights hidden in a clump of trees. He was talking nonsense. At the end, when I knew he was done for, he turned quiet and said: Am I going to hop it? I said: Not you, they'll take your arm off and you'll be quit of the war for good, damn you! It was what he wanted to hear, he believed me, it bucked him up. He went off like that.'

'Yes?'

'I came on the next night,' Murray said. 'I thought I had a chance to get through.'

'Where to?'

'Rheims, the Marne . . . wherever the French are going to stand.'

'They won't stand,' Ward said drily.

'But they must!' Murray said.

Ward shrugged his shoulders. 'I doubt it. A nation that has condemned itself in advance says must at its own risk. The French didn't prepare for this war. Their forts were useless— and why?—simply because every time a child or an old man saw soldiers marching along the street, instead of smiling he thought: It mustn't happen. And every Frenchwoman when she opened her eyes in the morning, thought: It mustn't happen today. . . . Mustn't, not must. . . . Could you see a road from your clump of trees?'

'Yes.'

'What could you see?'

'Women, old people, children, dragging themselves from village to village, and ditch to ditch. All of them stupid with fear.'

'Exactly!' Ward said.

In the brief pause, Lucien Vidal turned and went noiselessly up the stairs. Neither of the others noticed him.

'How did you get here, sir?' Murray asked.

'I was hit in the knee after we left Arras. My servant brought me as far as here. Next thing I knew the Germans were in Beaucourt, tanks showed up on this side of the river, and I hopped down to the cellar. I was alone here for a week. This morning at two o'clock three Frenchmen turned up. All the dear Allies.'

'You can tell me what to do,' Murray said.

'The devil I can. You must push off tomorrow night. I'm surprised Broussard picked you up.'

'What chance is there of getting through?'

'Oh, none,' Ward said. 'It's useless to try

38

for the coast. I imagine everything has gone as far as Dieppe. The Germans are going to roll France up and lean it against the Maginot Line. I advise you to try for Bordeaux. You might get there in time.'

'What about you, sir?'

'I shall go tomorrow night. Not with you.'

'Why not?'

'My knee,' Ward said curtly. 'It ought to have healed quicker. Damn it, I'm getting old, I'm a war or two out of date.'

Murray was handling the crutches. 'You won't be able to get far on these.'

'Oh, quite,' Ward said.

'I see.'

'I doubt whether you see anything of importance,' Ward said drily.

'I could give you a hand. . . .'

'Thanks. I shan't need it. . . . You could take a letter, if I write one. Suppose I turned up after all—when they imagined they'd seen the last of me. Embarrassing. Besides, what am I to say? . . . We left Arras on such and such a day and fought there and at Beaurains, and I was hit and lost the whole of my baggage, and the colonel was hit. . . . It hardly seems worth interrupting people's conversation to tell them that.'

Murray did not answer. He had listened with a young polite interest. He stood up and looked about him.

'Not bad here.'

'Your name startled me,' Ward said. 'I was here, in this cellar, in 1916, with a man called Murray. James Murray. It's odd you should walk in with his surname. You have a look of him. He was my age. I mean we were the same age in 1916. . . . I'm beginning to talk nonsense, like your Cockney friend.'

'I'm afraid we're not second cousins,' Murray said, smiling.

'He used to write poems about his part of England. Somewhere west, I think.'

Murray stifled a yawn. 'Mathematics is my trick. If the war had held off another year. . . . Though since we knew it was coming, it was almost a relief. People were talking about it over my head when I was a child. I remember looking for it in part of the garden. When I went to school we used to argue when, not if.'

'Clever of you,' Ward said. 'We didn't notice ours until it arrived.'

Murray smiled. 'Not so clever.'

'Not at all,' Ward said. 'You knew about this war because we told you.'

'Then why didn't you tell us how to escape?'

'Men who ought to know told us it wouldn't happen. They were lending the Germans money to keep them quiet. . . . In any case you have no right to blame us.'

'Did you expect us to clear up your mess?' Murray said coldly. 'You remind me of a boring old fool who made us a long speech about bombing planes in my last year at school. Young men, he said, would fly them, and so young men would be responsible for killing people with the bombs. Lazy old humbug. Why did you let him get away with it?'

'No doubt you're right. . . . I'm not trying to excuse us. . . . After four years of war all we wanted was to sleep with our wives, a job, something to drink, perhaps have children.'

'Well, you had twenty years,' Murray said.

'Yes. But did we do anything with them?'

'You know best,' Murray said.

'Damn it, what are you deluding yourself you can do after this war—if you still exist? Do you, yes, you, d'you expect peace to last fifty years?'

'I don't expect anything,' Murray said. 'All I hope is to be left to get on with my work. Politics bore me.'

'You're not a toss better than we were.'

'No. But you thought you'd finished something. It didn't occur to you that peace is an unusual accident, and can't last.'

'You might try to beat that,' Ward said.

'Yes. I think we ought to occupy Germany for twenty years. It will take them another twenty to re-arm.'

'And the war will be fought by your children.'

'Oh, I shan't have any,' Murray said with a smile.

'And the English will die out.'

'It's ridiculous,' Murray said calmly. 'You and your friends, I've read their books, rushed into the last war as though it had been hand-made for you. Some of you were still pleased with it when you were killed. After a year or two the rest knew the war had been made for lice, speculators, politicians, staff captains, rats. You were vexed because you'd been deceived and deceived yourselves. You didn't leave us any useful illusions.'

'Why are you here?'

'I don't like Germans. Not these Germans. But war is a nuisance. If it happens too often it's time for families to stop.'

'No, you're not like Jamie,' Ward said.

'Sorry,' Murray said, smiling.

'Queer—it's only since this war started that I miss him acutely,' Ward said. 'I was sorry at the time—but it didn't last. I knew what I was going to do at the end of the war, I had a few ambitions, I thought comfortably about the future. When he was killed I imagined his place filled, his place in the future. By someone. By me, perhaps. There would always be some-one to eat roast lamb and spring potatoes and drink claret. And walk, sleep, look at women. So I thought. But the last weeks, in fact since we came back here, on these roads, in villages I knew the names of as well as I know the names of my friends, in this cellar, I've known for certain that a country is poorer for every young man killed fighting and every child murdered by a bomb. And that the debt will be paid. . . . I've suffered for the first time because Jamie was killed. With his illusions, his quiet laugh, his young selfishness, his hopes. The young men of his age who are going to disappear in this war won't even talk about the same things.'

'Are you sure?' Murray said. 'Rain, cold, the heat of these last weeks, the idea of being hit, shouldn't I agree with your friend about that?'

'You didn't live in the same country. . . . England before the last war . . . you don't know what it was like. The stillness of the country, the slowness of time in country gardens, the slow train journeys to places that didn't alter. My dear boy, you don't know what's lost.'

'You idealise it, of course,' Murray said.

'Oh, quite.'

'The first thing I shall do when I get back is to ask my mother where she found her gardening scissors. She puts things under cushions and forgets them.'

'I shall go north,' Ward said. 'You can see thirty miles and four rivers on a clear day from my attic.'

'If this weather holds till you get back,' Murray began.

He stopped abruptly.

'It will be any weather I choose,' Ward said. He took his notebook out of his pocket, and a pencil, and prepared to write. 'You'd better get some sleep.'


6


Murray walked over to the bench and looked at it with an awkward indecision. He turned round at a slight noise. The hatch at the top of the stairs had been lifted; Lucien Vidal came down the stairs, carrying a foot or so of bread, a bottle of wine, three glasses. He looked back at the foot of the stairs.

'Thank you, Martine.'

The hatch was gently closed.

'Will you have a drink, sir?' Vidal asked Major Ward. 'It's red.'

'No, thanks.'

'Do you mind if we do?'

'No, no, go ahead,' Ward said.

He returned, frowning, to his letter.

'Oh, it's you,' Murray said.

Vidal laughed. 'I recognised you at once.'

'September 1937, Paris. Do you remember my bedroom?'

'My God, it was ordinary enough,' Vidal said.

'When I leaned far enough out I could see the Panthéon on my left and on the right the trees of the Luxembourg. Not to speak of a shabby fountain. Perfect.'

'Why not? There are hundreds of fountains in Paris.'

'It was gloriously hot. There were people going to work before six every morning, at six a girl used to run past. I could have touched her. A boy delivering rolls as long as an umbrella tucked them under his arm and disappeared into the pissoir. And my God the light was strong.'

'I noticed it went to your head,' Vidal said.

'And Bella? What happened about her?' Murray asked.

'Nothing. I broke it off.'

'Why?'

'These aren't times to get involved, least of all seriously.'

Major Ward lit the candle that was standing on the table. He put his pocketbook and pencil away, got up painfully, candle in hand, and limped off on his crutches, dragging one leg, to the cellar on the left. The young men noticed he was going. Murray, who was sitting down, half rose, and at Ward's furious hand-wave, dropped back into his chair. Before Ward had limped out of sight they had forgotten him.

'And your writing?' Murray said.

'No good either,' Vidal said gloomily.

'Why not?'

'Oh, I was out of step with the others. I detest quarrelling, and writers do nothing else nowadays. A few of them were honest men, they rushed off to Spain and got killed. The others made use of Spain, as they make use of everything, of the poor, the sick, the miserable, the conscientious, to set up a romantic legend of themselves and make excuses for being well-off or cowards. Even in Spain they quarrelled dishonestly over the dead Spaniards, and wrote poetry to prove that those who died facing west were saints, and the others, all who died facing the east, were liars and murderers. It's the new technique.'

'I don't read either,' Murray said.

'You needn't. Both sides cheat. There's only one honest writer and he's still doing what he began trying to do centuries ago. Slipping across frontiers to see for himself that we drink, eat, sleep with our wives, in the same way in all languages. You notice that every time we forget it we become stupider than usual. As we have now. . . . Let me fill your glass.'

'You should write what you want to.'

'I do,' Vidal said. 'And I make a parcel of the manuscript and post it to myself with a refusal.'

'Coward.'

'I don't cheat. At the end of the room where the man is dying I put a young woman with a round neck, red strong hands and a smooth face. Just as it's no use describing a cruel scene if you forget to put in the dog enjoying itself in the corner. Don't you see? You can bet someone's comfortably asleep in your room in Paris at this moment and will wake up in that light while you're stifling here. Think of it!'

'Think of the months this war has wasted,' Murray said.

'You should improve yourself in your spare time. . . . What were you going to do?'

'Join a flying club, marry, live in the country.'

'I meant your work,' Vidal said.

'Real mathematics. Nothing to do with war or politics. The most peaceably selfish and single-minded life possible.'

'Really? You're lucky,' Vidal said. 'Everything I wanted to do was doubled by a fear or a hatred. I was going to write, but it meant taking sides in a quarrel between Frenchmen. A murderous quarrel. . . . Even the thought of marriage . . . We should have been poor. You have no idea what a handicap it is to have Catholic parents. . . . When the war started I was thankful. No more doubts. Only one thing to hate—Germany. And only one fear. . . . I thought I might be afraid. . . . Well, it was as simple as that for a few months, a few days, perhaps only a few seconds. I came back from leave, from Paris, the restaurants there were crowded with Jews eating and drinking and laughing, and the first creature I saw when I left the train was a child standing with bare feet in the cold, crying with cold. And in Paris the politicians were up to all their old tricks, lying, cheating, ruining each other. What conceivable link is there between them and my foul-mouthed innocent soldiers, defenceless when it comes to policies, profits, and the jealousies of the politicians in Paris. If they'd been told they were fighting to get back their sour cabbage and omelette they would have marched just as willingly. They were told to save their country. Which, I ask you, which country? The one I knew in the battalion and the one in Paris are about as like each other as living and dead.'

'Save them one at a time,' Murray said.

'When you go on leave, don't you feel that England is two countries? One you love and one you only detest?'

'Certainly not. Besides, I'm interested in saving a couple of fields and the best trout river in England.'

'You don't know the best in France!' Vidal exclaimed. 'Wait until you've lived in Beynac in summer. Wait and see the Dordogne, doubled by the sun, wait until you hear and smell our lime-trees, doubled by bees. Wait until you've tried the wine we grow ourselves.'

'Doubled, too, I hope.'

Vidal lifted his glass. 'Salut!'

'Cheers! If I had to stick to one meal for the rest of my life I should make it wine and French bread.'

'There's something to be said for coffee, rolls, and honey.'

'Yes, but for that you want the sun,' Murray said.

A young woman, very young, sunburned, dark-haired and dark-eyed, had come silently down the steps, leaving the hatch open. They only heard her when she came into the cellar.

'Martine!' Vidal exclaimed.

'I came to see if you wanted anything. Some more bread?'

'Very weak,' Vidal said, smiling. 'You told me this was the last of the bread until you make. You came to look at him.'

Martine looked at the young Englishman. 'No.'

Murray didn't say anything. Less at his ease with her than Vidal, he leaned against the table and watched intently.

Vidal touched her arm lightly and briefly. 'How warm you are, Martine.'

50

Martine was still looking at the Englishman
with the wary dignity of a child. 'I was working
in the field all morning and this evening. The
heat is like a quilt. There was no wind. . . .
They say Arras is still burning. Is it true? My
father believes everything and nothing. He says
the Germans will win, they won't win, they'll
take everything, they'll leave us the fields. He
can't make himself believe they'll take ours.'

'I know you oughtn't to stay in the farm,'
Vidal said.

'Why not?'

'You're off any main road and the Germans
are busy, but they won't always be busy and they
won't forget to visit you.'

'They won't hurt me,' Martine said.

Vidal frowned. 'Nonsense.'

'Why should they?'

'You know as well as I do what they're like,
and so did your mother and her mother.'

'One thing I can do if a German comes here,'
Martine said in a light voice. 'When I look him
full in the eyes I shall see a German girl. I shall
guess from that what to say to him to make him
respectful.'

'German women have yellow hair, they're broad
and three times your height,' Vidal said. 'Giants.'

'Very well, my hair will be another protection. Not to speak of my brown skin.'

She shook her hair forward and glanced quickly at Murray.

'You look very pretty like that,' Vidal said.

'My cousin said so.'

'Where is he?'

'Oh, at the war.'

'Martine, you're in love with him.'

'No.'

'Then why,' Vidal said, 'did you speak about him?'

'He came into my mind.'

'I wonder what your mind is like. Let me look.' He leaned forward to look into her eyes. 'Yes, I can see fields, the sky, a corner of the Ancre. But no cousin.'

'I'm not thinking of him,' Martine said, smiling.

'Which of us were you thinking of?' Vidal jerked his head at Murray. 'You've known me a day longer.'

'Neither of you.'

'We shan't be here tomorrow. Think about us then. I shall think of you in this cellar.'

'Why? I'm always in the fields or the kitchen. I prefer the fields. You can't think how empty this house is without a worn step or a single old chair or looking-glass. I've scratched some of them, for my daughter to find.'

They heard voices in the yard suddenly. Martine listened a moment, then hurried off. The young men watched her run quickly up the stairs. She dropped the hatch.

'Do you sleep down here?' Murray said, with an air of constraint. 'It's very airless.'

'We got here this morning and slept in there.' Vidal nodded towards the cellar on the left. 'The English officer sleeps here. You could sleep in the yard.'

### 7

The hatch was flung noisily back. Captain Redon came down the steps, pushing in front of him a young German. Pierre Masson followed. The noise they made brought Ward back into the middle cellar.

'What have you got there?' he said.

'He pitched off his motor-cycle into the ditch,' Redon said, 'right on our heads. I thought he'd broken my neck. His machine hit something in the road. He must have been doing ninety.'

'This is rather a bore, isn't it?' Ward said, frowning. 'What are we to do with him?'

'Your name?' Redon asked the German.

'Richard Langer.'

'Regiment?'

The German was silent.

'Where have you come from?'

Silence.

'Where were you going?'

'On duty,' Langer said.

'Go through his things,' Redon ordered Masson.

Masson threw one thing after another on the table.

'Letter. A piece of string. An excellent knife. Photographs. First aid.'

Redon took the letter up and unfolded it.

'It is written by my mother,' the young German said coldly.

'I don't read German,' Redon said.

'I can,' Murray said.

Redon noticed him for the first time. 'Who's this?'

'A survivor, don't worry, I vouch for him,' Ward said, with a little impatience. Redon handed over the letter and Murray looked through it quickly.

'It is from his mother,' he said.

'May I have it back?' Langer asked.

Redon took the letter from the young Englishman and laid it on the table.

'How many German troops are in this sector now?' he said.

'Is it likely I should tell you, if I knew?' the German said loudly.

Ward noticed that he was less self-controlled than he was trying to seem.

'Your advanced troops were able to reach the Marne at one point,' Redon said.

'Oh, yes?'

'They failed badly and they're retreating in a hurry.'

'A lie,' Langer said excitedly. 'We crossed the Marne yesterday, we're in Rheims and Châlons. We shall be in Paris tomorrow.'

'Your leaders may have reasons for lying to you. We shall see,' Redon said placidly.

The German was on the edge of a breakdown. 'No one lies to us, I tell you,' he said.

'You were taking a short cut to Amiens. Had you a message?' Redon said.

The German tried to jump at him and was dragged back by Masson and the young Englishman.

'Kill me,' he said. He began to weep as he struggled. 'I deserve to be shot. I couldn't face him again, I've failed, kill me.'

'We'll go on when you're not hysterical,' Redon said very coldly. He picked up one of the photographs, holding it to the lamp.

'Hitler?' Ward asked.

'Yes, of course. All these youths carry it about with them. You won't find it so often on an old soldier.' He took up the second photograph. 'This is more human.'

Ward looked at it. 'I should think his mother.'

'He's crying for her,' Masson said in a jeering voice.

'Hold your tongue,' Redon said. He asked Ward whether he wanted to ask the German any questions.

'It's hardly worth it,' Ward said, 'I'm not interested in his devotions.'

The young German had recovered his self-control.

'Are you ready to listen?' Redon said to him. 'If it helps you, remember you're talking to a Frenchman. All this revivalism is out of place.'

'The French are cowards,' Langer said.

'Can we decide what we're going to do with him?' Ward said quietly.

Redon spoke to Langer in a flat voice. 'If we release you, tomorrow morning or at once, will you give us your word of honour to say nothing? And nothing about this farm?'

'His word,' Pierre Masson said softly.

'Well?'

'No,' Langer said. 'The French are liars.'

Ward let his hand fall on the table. 'I suppose we can't tie him up and leave him, to take his chance.'

'You're not thinking what you're saying,' Redon said. 'D'you expect Broussard to keep him here? As soon as we left he'd release him if he thought that was the safest thing to do. Or kill him to make sure.'

'Yes, yes. Why the hell didn't he break his neck in your ditch?'

'If you won't give us your word, what are we to do with you?' Redon said to Langer.

Langer did not speak.

'It's simple enough,' Redon said gravely.

'May I have my letter?' Langer said. 'And the two photographs.'

Redon gave them to him.

'Why not sleep on it?' Ward said irritably.

'You think . . .? No, what's the good of that? You're putting off a decision we should have to come to in a few hours. I don't follow you.'

'Sleeping on it is a rule in my family.'

'I see . . . you're superstitious.'

'One rule is as good as another in this hopelessly irregular business,' Ward said.

'It's unfortunate but it's not irregular,' Redon said calmly. 'I can't say I want to wait another twenty-four hours in this cellar—which is what it would mean.'

'I daresay we have plenty of time. . . . I ask you to sleep on it.'

'Very well. But—and I ask you to note—it's against my better judgement.'

'Thanks,' Ward said. 'I may be able to think of a way out.'

'He must have a guard.' Redon looked first at Masson and then at Vidal. 'Which of them can I trust?'

'Can you keep awake?' Ward asked Murray.

'Yes, easily.'

'Call your dogs off,' Ward said, 'I'll lend you mine.'

'Right. . . . But I think we'll keep him in one place. I like a tidy room.'

He told Masson to tie the German to the

bench. Masson took the rope from the nail where it was hanging with the set of harness. Between them he and Murray fastened Langer's wrists together in front, and his ankle to a leg of the bench.

'Don't overdo it,' Redon said.

'I shall sleep in there,' Ward told Murray. He nodded towards the cellar on the left.

'He'll be all right,' Murray said easily.

'We shall be in the yard or the kitchen.' Redon looked at the two young Frenchmen. 'You can go.'

Masson followed him towards the stairs. Vidal took a step, hesitated, stood still.

Redon turned, and waited. 'Get on,' he said.

# CHAPTER II

## I

RICHARD MURRAY looked at his wrist-watch and involuntarily at the shaft, closed. He knew that, outside, the difference between night, the short June night, and dawn, the dawn that sent him hurrying into some wood or barn, must be marked already. Hard to believe it. What light there was in the cellar came from the lamp. He tried turning it up. He lifted it to look at the prisoner, who was asleep. His head hung forward, so low that his eyelids were a wrinkled line drawn across the absence of his eyes. Murray lowered the lamp, and its light fell across the prisoner's hands, pallid and hanging. As he turned to replace the lamp on the table, the German roused, with a grimace of misery. Murray turned round and saw the other looking at him. It gave him a curious shock, as though a mask of flesh had suddenly been removed.

'Uncomfortable?' he asked.

'My wrists and leg,' Langer said.

'Give me your word to sit still, I'll untie you.'

'You English are all like schoolboys,' Langer said contemptuously. 'Give me your word, be kind to dumb animals, don't tell tales. All the old dust of your houses.'

Murray yawned. 'If you'd rather be uncomfortable.'

There was a short silence.

'Perhaps if you ask me again . . .' Langer said.

'I shan't ask you,' Murray said pleasantly. 'You'll ask me.'

'I won't.'

'It suits me,' Murray said.

After a moment the German said quietly, 'I give you my word.'

'Sensible fellow,' Murray said.

He knelt and loosened the ankle rope a little, then freed the German's wrists completely. At the table he held the bottle of wine against the lamp.

'There's a little left. Will you have it?'

'Please,' Langer said.

'And an inch of bread.'

'Please. Bread and wine. . . . You speak better German than I can speak French, although I learned it thoroughly. To be ready to give orders.'

'That must put a brake on conversation.'

'Excuse me?' Langer said.

61

'A joke,' Murray said.

'Why did you learn German?' Langer asked patiently.

'I spent a year in Munich. I was living with a professor of history who used to tell me that the English are really Germans but we deteriorated when we gave up breeding geese.'

Langer's face changed. 'Munich! You must have seen the Leader.'

'Yes. I did,' Murray said. 'Once.'

'Oh my God, how I envy you,' Langer said. 'I've never seen him. Only the films.'

'Pity . . . if you're keen.'

'I missed my chance. I had measles the year he came to a town eight miles from our village.'

'Where do you live?'

'Ostermünde. No, you never heard of it. It's on the Baltic coast. There's a harbour, a street with shops, the market-square, the school and two churches. The sand blows in everywhere, under all the doors. There are pines, of course. The best month is in summer, when you can swim as far as the lighthouse, and the sun coming off the water in your eyes makes you shut them, you have to swim blind.'

'It's five years since I was in Germany,' Murray said.

'Ah, then you don't really know how strong we're making it. I say we, because I help.'

Murray wanted to be polite. 'What were you doing?'

'I'd just—last July—taken a scholarship. I was going to Berlin in the autumn, to specialise in mathematics.'

'Good, that's my subject,' Murray said. 'I'd make everybody learn mathematics, whether they wanted to or not. Simply to clear out their minds.'

'You make me laugh,' Langer said, 'you're so childish. German mathematics has to serve the Leader, like everything else. What use is anything if it doesn't? What use are any of us except to him? We get up for him at five, winter and summer, we harden ourselves, we study science, history, mathematics, we have as many children as we can, we die . . . everything is for him. It's natural.'

'Oh, yes?' Murray said. 'And when you swim in the Baltic, and the sun in your eyes blinds you, are you doing that for Hitler?'

'In a way.'

'What way?'

'Yes. I do it for him,' Langer said.

'I'm glad to say that George Six isn't so

63

exacting, I can swim or eat honey on my bread-and-butter without going into a patriotic trance.'

'The English are not altogether worthless, they're weakened by self-indulgence.'

'Thanks for the flowers.'

'Excuse me?'

'I don't agree with you,' Murray said. 'I feel all the better for eating the honey and I can give it up when I like.'

'I don't want to annoy you,' Langer said anxiously. 'The English are brave, of course. Some of you are brave. At any rate, you're not Frenchmen. It's a pity you didn't join us, then our army could have taught yours, you would have had the Leader as your leader—we should have won every war. . . . You'd be like me. I'm nobody. Langer the son of Langer the police-man, from Ostermünde. Hitler makes me a hundred times stronger than I am, it's exactly as if he took hold of my arm and told me what to do. If he told me to follow him to hell I should go. Yes, and thankfully.'

'Have it your own way,' Murray said. 'I like to look where I'm going.'

'I'm sorry for you!' Langer said quickly. 'I pity any country where people have to choose for themselves what to believe. Ordinary men and women who only want to be loved and kept in order, even if it does mean a thrashing now and then. You know, my father thrashed me from the first day I could stand.'

'Poor little Boche,' Murray said.

'Say it,' Langer said bitterly. 'Amuse yourself by insulting a prisoner.'

Murray smiled at him. 'No, no, don't be so touchy, I forgot you were a prisoner. I was thinking that you ought to die off at fourteen, the whole shoot of you. Do you ever have nightmares? I sometimes dream I'm back at school for eternity. Frightful. If the prefects were allowed to carry whips, and if the head had been cracky with ambition, if the whole place had been clean and frightening and you couldn't laugh even at the dottiest of the masters, and if you were kept repeating the same lessons . . . it must be very like Germany, according to you. And to crown all, you like it!'

'No. It isn't like that,' Langer said, sighing, 'it's beautiful.'

'To look at,' Murray said, 'I know, I've seen it.'

The German boy shook his head. 'To live in. . . . It wasn't, before he came. It was cold and ugly, a horror. No one helped us. But now—now—we have him to reward us when we do well. No one is lonely. We have our comrades, we eat together, we march out singing like one man, one young Hitler man. Besides, you don't know what it was like before he came. One day I remember is the day my mother wanted to buy me a pair of shoes. As soon as my father came in she took all his wages and ran with them to the shop, but the shoes were dearer again than the day before, the money wasn't enough, and it was the same next week when he gave her more money, the shoes were more money, always a little way in front of us, a mirage. And all this time my feet were tied up in a piece of her dress and then in newspaper. At last she cried in front of the shoemaker and said, Look at his feet, look at my child, is it right he should be dying of cold when his father and I work, doesn't anyone care about us? . . . It was before our Leader came, I was three.'

'All I remember,' Murray said, 'from my third year, is being given a strawberry to eat and spitting it out.'

'You see, you had everything,' Langer said. 'And you stole everything from us.'

'Not me.'

'You'll have to pay for it along with the rest,'

Langer said fiercely. 'You starved us, you told us lies, and preached to us. Now it's our turn, and when your wife is crying over her child you can tell her, yes, it's justice. The justice of the Germans. Of the Boches if you like.'

'Splendid. But for the moment I shall call you poor little Boche.'

'You always under-rated us.'

'Not at all,' Murray said. 'And I don't like you and I'm not laughing at you. And I shouldn't forgive you if you defeated us, or if you make us suffer, and if you dive-bomb my village, and if you tried to turn my children when I have any into inferior Boches. And I don't admire you in the least for driving your tanks over cathedrals and poor little brats' toys and wheat-fields and pieces of flesh. But, in spite of all that, since I'm not older or better than you are and what's more to the point I was happy in Munich, I'm nearly indifferent, I don't hate you, I only wish you weren't so excitable. . . . Look at your hands.'

Langer opened his clenched hands slowly.

'You've made them bleed. Why?'

Langer smiled. 'No, you don't like me, and you don't understand the Germans.'

'I knew we should come to that!' Murray said.

'Why didn't you stay in Munich? You would have seen the health come back to our country, with the flags and songs, and the happiness of having something hard and splendid to do.'

'Pity you can't see Stockbridge,' Murray said. 'Some of us have been doing the same job for five or six hundred years. . . . I won't pretend we go in much for, what was it? splendid hardness, but we breed a few horses, and plough as near the edge of the Downs as we can, and keep our beech hedges in order—they say the Romans planted them—and discuss our neighbours. We keep our hopes and fears strictly to ourselves, and only exchange them in times of crisis, together with recipes from the last war. I was ten years old before I saw a flag. You should come and look at us.'

'Yes,' Langer said, 'I should like it, I should be happy, and want to live there for ever. We should make plans to see each other again, and next month war would break out.'

'It proves how fatuous war is.'

'Not at all. If it proves anything it proves the inevitability of wars—since not even goodwill stops them.'

'No. One of us must have been telling lies.'

Langer burst out laughing. 'Never mind—

you're a good chap. If you weren't I should have made a bolt for it.'

He stretched out his leg, to show that he had worked his foot out of the loosened rope.

'You gave me your word not to move,' Murray said calmly.

'I did. And if it was my duty to bolt I should bolt. Certainly I ought to try. Why don't I?'

'Because I should shoot you.'

'That's not the only reason,' the German said slowly. 'Nor the little Frenchmen snoring up there.'

'I suppose you have some hard splendid reason.'

'Not exactly. . . . Would you believe me if I said I like you? It doesn't mean anything. If I could get away by killing you, I should kill you. It's what he would expect me to do. But I should be sorry.'

'Nice of you.'

'No, you don't understand,' Langer said quickly.

Murray leaned forward. 'Tell me. Do you trust anybody?'

'Our Leader——'

Murray interrupted him. 'Yes, yes, quite, but your friends, do you trust your friends?'

'Why don't you listen?' Langer cried. 'I trust him, I tell you. All my loyalty, like my eyesight, my mind, and my life, has to be for him. And he trusts all of us men, oh and I suppose women, who follow him to the death. It's what makes us harder than you.'

'And more splendid. . . . I suppose a savage would feel the same things about his chief. Stupid of me, but I like to feel I can trust the man next me.'

'Never mind it now,' Langer said, smiling. 'You're going to shoot me in a few minutes— less than an hour—which is savage enough.'

'You were given your chance.'

'Yes, you gave me the chance to save myself by denying him. . . .'

'Haven't you done enough showing off?' Murray said quickly.

'Oh, if you're going to call it that,' Langer said.

'Call it anything you like, tell me it's your spiritual exercises, it's all the same to me. But you're wasting time.'

The German looked at him. 'You mean I haven't much longer?' he said quickly.

'As a matter of fact, my watch has stopped,' Murray lied. 'I forgot to wind it.'

'You remind me of my half-brother. I used to wait for him when I was small, I suppose he was about twenty-five then, he'd been a soldier, he had the Iron Cross, he used to run with me on his shoulders and give me little boats he made for me. You see he couldn't get any work and he had no money. But he was always the same, always without respect. Even when he heard the Leader he laughed, and when I was thirteen we quarrelled. I don't know what's become of him.'

'He would certainly tell you you're a fool to commit suicide.'

'Will you send off a letter to my mother?'

'Yes.'

'Have you a sheet of paper?'

Murray looked in his pockets. Nothing. He had his back to the table. Suddenly Langer caught sight of a piece of paper Major Ward had left lying there. He jumped up and reached for it. Murray sprang at him at once and pushed him roughly on to the bench.

'You hurt me,' Langer said reproachfully.

'Your own fault.'

Langer shook his head. 'No. You hurt me, myself. I'd forgotten where I am.'

'Sorry,' Murray said curtly. 'I apologise.'

Langer smiled. 'You needn't. I should play a trick on you if I thought it would come off. That doesn't mean I don't respect you.'

'Thanks!'

'You don't believe me. I scarcely believe myself. Why don't I hate you? My father used to tell me the English are the meanest, the most hypocritical, the greediest race in the world, worse than the French, who are only rotten. I suppose your father taught you the same about us.'

'My father read the German poets and preferred German cooking to English. He told me Germany is a magnificent country, and the Germans the most devoted and the simplest of savages, he said we ought to conquer them, then forgive them, then civilise them. He adored Germany.'

'So it seems!'

Murray picked up the sheet of paper on the table, glanced at it and laid it down.

'I'm afraid this is part of a letter,' he said. 'I can't give it to you.'

'Never mind. If I give you a message, will you memorise it, and if you're not killed will you go and see my mother after the war and repeat it to her?'

72

Murray frowned. 'Is she the sort of person who'd want to see me?'

'Oh yes,' Langer said eagerly. 'She's small, with small features, not like me. She hasn't had a new dress, not entirely new, I mean—a new collar, perhaps, or a new top, but not the whole dress—since I remember. She's quick-tempered. And she puts things under cushions and forgets them.'

Murray's face contracted with grief and horror. 'The stupidity of this war,' he said in a low voice.

'It only seems stupid to you because you're going to lose,' the German said. 'You English have no faith in your country, you don't see it with the towns full of healthy boys and girls, all laughing, all with red cheeks and white teeth. You don't imagine what Germany promises to a German. If you'd kept out of our way you would have been safe, but you were so stupid you threatened us. Us! Do you know what you are, you're the past threatening the future? Everything in us answers you. Ostermünde, our smallest village. Our poorest scholar—me! And I don't hate you, when you gave me that wine and bread I even loved you. . . . You hate this war because you have none of our reasons for winning it.'

73

'Our reasons wouldn't appeal to you,' Murray said.

'Tell me one, one!'

'You boast.'

'So do you.'

'Sometimes. And then a voice at the back of the room, someone nobody ever heard of, makes a rude noise, and that tears it.'

'You're still boasting.'

'Never mind,' Murray said gently. 'Think of the sort of life we could have had. You'd be living in a German town smelling of coffee and cigars, and with luck I'd be in Cambridge, both of us working on the same thing, settled, married, a little bored perhaps but with plenty to think about. We should have met at a conference in some German city and drunk German wine together, and walked along clean decent streets and you would have pointed out a fourteenth-century house with the sun on it, and we should have agreed that mathematics is the perfect science, and Bach or Mozart—according to the wine we had had for lunch—the greatest musician. Or you would have supported Mozart and I Bach. And we should both have been right.'

The German closed his eyes. 'You know what to say to trap me. You're cleverer than I am.'

'If we shoot you———'

'When,' Langer said.

'What will you regret most when we shoot you?'

'That I hadn't time to do more for our glorious Leader———'

'No, no, think, think,' Murray said. 'You haven't long.'

'You have no right,' the German said.

'What?'

'To torture me.'

'Tell me. I'll pay you back.'

The German let both his hands, open, fall on his knee. 'I didn't finish my thesis. And this summer I was going to Bavaria . . . you know, I've never seen mountains, the country round Ostermünde is very flat. Like this.'

'Good,' Murray said softly.

'Your turn.'

'Do I know?'

'You're farther off than I am,' Langer said, touching him. 'But try to see it.'

'What?'

'The moment when——you don't remember that it's the last five seconds——when you touch something with your hand, and when you forget that in four seconds every tree in the world will have

75

vanished, when you think: I didn't look at the sea though I was living close to it. I didn't hear. I didn't see. My God, I didn't know there were so many thoughts in my head.'

'I'd scarcely begun my work,' Murray said.

Both of them heard footsteps and voices overhead, in the kitchen.

'Don't think I regret the war,' Langer said hurriedly. 'I'm only sorry I shall miss the end, with the people cheering and laughing in the streets. I should have enjoyed that.'

2

Major Ward limped in from the cellar on the left. He scarcely glanced at the young men, but the German sat up stiffly.

'But it's still dark,' Murray said.

'It's three-thirty. Getting light now outside. . . . You undid his wrists.'

'They were hurting him,' Murray said.

'Don't take on yourself to alter an order again.'

Captain Redon came down, carrying a candle he blew out, and snuffed the wick between his thumb and finger, when he came into the cellar.

'Well?' he said, 'did you sleep on it?'

76

'I slept.'

Redon nodded. 'I knew you would.'

'Listen carefully to me,' Ward said to the German. 'You're in an impossible position——'

Langer interrupted respectfully: 'I beg your pardon. There are positions where it's easy to do your duty and others where it's very difficult, but your duty is the same always.'

'Yes, yes, never mind that,' Ward said. 'Your position is that you've been captured, you're alone, you can't fight back, nor can you escape. What you can do is to give us your word to keep your head shut about this farm. You can give it without disgracing yourself. We're all leaving here, and you won't tell me that bringing trouble on a farmer and his daughter, both innocent, is part of your duty. . . . Suppose you'd pitched off your motor-cycle into an empty ditch. . . . Very well, you lay there stunned for a few hours. And now you get up and walk back to your company, and you carry on with your duty.'

'My duty is to kill Frenchmen . . .' Langer said.

'Oh, quite. But at the moment you can't, you can only be killed.'

'And if I give you my word,' Langer said slowly, 'nothing else, you'll let me off?'

'But you will——'

Murray stopped.

Langer smiled and spoke quickly. 'Why don't you say it?'

'I put it to you as a very much senior officer,' Captain Redon said. 'You will be shot, now, unless you promise me as a soldier to hold your tongue.'

Murray spoke hastily and loudly. 'His duty to Hitler won't let him keep any promises he makes us. Ask him.'

'I see we do understand each other,' the German said softly.

Ward looked at him. 'Isn't your word as a German worth anything?'

'A German soldier only gives his word to Hitler,' Langer said. 'Anything else is a disgrace.'

'You can trust me when I tell you there's no disgrace,' Redon said. 'I should give the same advice to my son if I had one.'

'Keep your advice for a Frenchman,' Langer said. 'I have the happiness to serve the Leader. I——'

Ward interrupted coldly. 'We can remember the rest.'

'The French are done for,' Langer shouted,

'they can't get any children, they're all cowards. It's all I have to say. Is it enough? Heil Hitler!'

Captain Redon looked at Ward. 'The original mistake was bringing him here.'

'Yes, why did you do it?'

They ignored the two young men: who waited, now and then looking at each other.

'He was dazed and I forgot for a second that he wasn't a casual accident. Afterwards I hesitated. It was a gross mistake.'

'You don't know the farm, do you?' Ward said.

'It was too dark to see much of it when we came.'

'I remember it very well,' Ward said, 'too well. . . . If you take the cart-track out of the yard and follow it for a hundred yards and turn left, past a small well, you'll find a sunken road— part of a communication trench in 1916.'

'Thanks.'

'Do you need me?'

'No. . . . I'm responsible.'

Ward looked at the German. 'You young fool,' he said kindly.

The hatch Redon had closed behind him was flung up, and the two young Frenchmen came down the stairs, leaving it open.

'Stand at the top of the stairs,' Redon ordered

Masson. Masson went back, taking his revolver in his hand as he went.

Ward spoke to Murray in an undertone. 'You'll stay here.'

'You're behaving admirably,' Redon said to the German. 'I regret all this very much.'

'Don't excuse yourself,' the German said.

'My poor child,' Redon said, 'I was speaking to you as an equal. Please go upstairs.'

'You didn't give me the message,' Murray said.

'Tell her what you like,' Langer said. 'Anything you think proper.'

He went upstairs. Redon followed him. After a brief pause, Major Ward picked up the piece of paper from the table, glanced at it, and put it in his pocket. He limped back to the cellar he had just left.

'Don't flatter yourself you could have done anything else,' he said angrily.

Murray and Lucien Vidal looked at him in silence.


3

As soon as he had gone, Vidal spoke.

'Why the sunken road?'

'Keeps the sound in.'

'Stupid of me. . . . What sort of a night did you have?'

'Quite all right. He slept most of the time.'

'Did he talk?' Vidal asked.

'Yes. I did him down afterwards.'

'What do you mean?'

'He talked rather frankly. Among other things he told me he would always break any parole he might give: his duty to Hitler comes before anything as human and seditious as a private scruple.'

'Well?'

'I passed his remarks on. It's queer, I don't believe he expected me to give him away.'

'You couldn't do anything else,' Vidal said.

'I daresay. . . . I'm sick of this war,' Murray said.

Vidal spread his hands out. 'Yes, I am, too.'

They heard two distant and half-muted shots, one and then after a brief pause the other.

'I don't know what difference there is between us and murderers,' Vidal said quietly and rapidly.

'No, it's the job,' Murray said. 'What d'you expect? It couldn't be helped. He pushed himself into our hands and we had to get rid of him, at the cost of a bad moment. What else could we have done? You tell me.'

Vidal drew down the corners of his mouth. 'This war will go on for years. The Germans have everything on their side, they're a machine made of aeroplanes, men, tanks, blind obedience. It will destroy France.'

'Only France?'

'It's enough!' Vidal exclaimed. 'I shan't waste any pity on other countries. Suppose Chartres is flattened out, suppose they burn the trees along the river at Beynac, suppose the twelfth-century wall I used to fish under is chucked into the water, suppose Paris is burned, and Albi, and Bordeaux and its quays? Suppose the vines are spoiled? But you have the heart to say: Only France? How like an ally.'

'Suppose my head is blown off,' Murray said.

'Chartres and your head are hardly on the same step,' Vidal said bitterly.

'No. Chartres can be put back.'

'I'm serious,' Vidal said.

'Do you think I'm not?' Murray said.

'You don't look it.'

'Good.'

'Don't make jokes,' Vidal said angrily. 'You only pretend to hate this war.'

'Nonsense. I'm not in the least romantic.

Unlike our war veterans.' Murray jerked his head in the direction of the invisible Ward. 'But what on earth does it matter what they feel at their age? Perhaps they needed excitement. I don't, I can invent my own. . . . Why think about your cathedrals and your precious trees if it frightens you? In any case it's too late. Why think at all, damn it? All that happens is that you imagine we're murderers because we had to kill a poor devil. . . .'

'And aren't we?'

'No, be reasonable, it's the war, not us. But if anyone likes war he must be dotty. I tell you, I only want to finish it. I want to get home and get on with my work.'

Pierre Masson had come quietly down the stairs. He stood in the doorway and listened. He was pale and he moistened his lips with his tongue before speaking.

'I knew you'd find your excuse for sentimentalising him,' he said with contempt. 'Poor devil, poor brave fellow . . . and the rest of it. . . . How like an Englishman.'

'Very like,' Murray said. 'Did you enjoy shooting him?'

'It was too easy, he didn't feel it.'

'Don't be an ass,' Murray said.

'No, look at him,' Vidal said. 'He's ashamed because he didn't enjoy it.'

Masson looked at him. 'You couldn't behave rationally sometimes?'

'Was he blindfolded? . . .' Vidal said.

'No. Captain Redon told him to walk on in front of us——'

Murray interrupted him calmly. 'That's enough, we can drop it. It's only fatuous to worry about one man. We're all in this, and you can't decently be sorry for anyone, it's too much like being sorry for yourself.'

Masson ignored him. Turning to Vidal he said, 'You maunder about the death of this wretched Boche and you'd only feel relief if every Frenchman who thinks as I do had been killed.'

'The air would certainly be purer in France.'

'We'll see what it's like after the war when your German friends have been chased out of the country,' Masson said.

Major Ward came in. He stood in the doorway, looking at them with contempt and dislike.

'Shut up,' he said. 'You're making a nuisance of yourselves.'

He went over to the table, turning his back on them. He moved the lamp, laid his piece of paper beside it, and turned round brusquely.

'Go on, get out of here. I can't stand hearing your voices any longer. Get away upstairs. Open the shutters when you go out.'

They went. He waited, standing, until the shutters were pulled back. Light came into the cellar. He sat down, turned the lamp out, and wrote little more than a line before pushing the paper aside. He began to talk to himself aloud. It was an old habit he no longer took the trouble to correct. What was the use?

'If I could have ten minutes' quiet talk with a sensible man. . . . What was it Jamie used to say about the French? They reminded him of a woman he knew and admired so much that he only hoped he would never see her again. . . . I'd thank you to tell me one thing, old boy. Weren't we a damn sight younger—or were we only simpler - minded—than this lot? I may be wrong, but I seem to remember us talking endlessly and childlessly all about our own little war, and about the rain, and about our chances of four days' leave. Things have changed since our day. . . . I suppose you don't remember this cellar? . . . I sharpened your knife for you on one of the steps. . . .'

He limped over to them and passed his hand up the side of the stairs.

'There's the place. . . . Think of that, will you! And next day, after all the trouble I'd taken, you were shabby enough to get yourself killed. Only a few minutes after you'd told me your father lived to be ninety-six and his father until he was eighty, so that the signs were in favour of you passing the century. . . . And here I am, and there you sat and warned me that you always cut yourself on a sharp knife.'

He turned clumsily, knocking his knee on one of the chairs.

'This damned knee will be the death of me. You'd have to laugh, wouldn't you? . . . Answer. . . .'

### 4

The hatch at the top of the stairs was opened gently. Captain Redon came down. Ward limped back to the table.

'Well?'

'Finished,' Redon said. 'It's a curious thing—you know I've no son, I never married—it's curious that the first feeling I ever had that might be the feeling a father has for his son, or I suppose it's that, should be for a German. Underneath his insolence, he was a good boy.'

'And stupid and a fanatic.'

'He'd been corrupted,' Redon said.

'Aren't we all corrupted—or coarsened at any rate—by war?'

'No. Not by war. By being taught—this boy had been taught—to deny the first thing he ought to have learned after he became a soldier. War is made up of cruelties and cruel decisions, it's an inhuman business. All the more reason for not boasting, and for keeping a promise.'

'He refused to make any promises.'

'He was going to,' said Redon, 'when your young man stopped him.'

'I wonder.'

'The less one wonders in this business the better,' Redon said.

Ward looked at him with curiosity. 'You're a professional soldier, of course?'

'My great-grandfather and my father were both soldiers. My father tried to make a doctor of me; he was vexed when I insisted on going into the army after all he had told me about the boredom and his own disappointments. I chose it deliberately. I knew I should be handicapped by poverty, I have no money of my own and no influence. You can see how little I've done for myself. I'm forty-eight. After this war I shall

be retired, with the pension of an infantry captain.
I'm not grumbling, I've had the impersonal life
I wanted, a life without little responsibilities.
And I can live on my pension.'

'Where will you go?'

'I have a house and a scrap of ground. They
came to me from my grandfather. It's out of
politeness to him that I call it a house, it has two
rooms and a shed. But it's on the Loire near
Orleans. You know the Loire, of course.'

'No.'

'It's a lazy wide river, full of sand-banks in
summer. It holds a remarkable quantity of light.
I've never seen a river that wasn't dull by com-
parison. Don't mistake me, I don't say it's the
handsomest river in the whole world——for that I
daresay you'd choose the Rhône or the Garonne.
But to know how much light the two banks of a river
can hold you need to have seen the Loire. It's something quite out of the common, even in France.'

'I'm sure of it,' Ward said.

'I have the right to fish off my quarter-acre. I
shall be able to afford a newspaper. I shall limit
myself in tobacco, and there are a few books in
the house. I read slowly. After a decent interval
I read the same books again. If they were worth
reading they don't blab everything at once.'

'How long have you been soldiering? All this seems a meagre reward.'

'I never expected a reward, or any thanks. I dislike being noticed. Anything I have done was for myself chiefly. All the same I should like—forgive me for talking about myself, it's not a habit, something has given way in me, perhaps the Marne—I should like a certain respect. I shall be happy if my neighbours treat me as a fellow-citizen, a man they can argue with over a glass of Vouvray. . . . They won't. . . .'

'Why not?' Ward said.

'I know the people I shall be living with—retired lawyers, civil servants, schoolmasters, a few farmers. Admirable people, friendly, suspicious, reserved. I shall be the odd number among them. Everything about me, my training as a soldier, my Catholic upbringing, rouses distrust in the only men I care to talk to, the retired schoolmaster and the librarian. In the end I shall find it simpler to keep to myself.'

'It didn't occur to me that you're a Catholic,' Ward said.

Redon made a slight gesture. 'I'm not a believing Catholic. I haven't the persistence—or is it vanity one needs?—to think much about eternal life. I've had to think about my duty as a perpetual soldier. . . . It hasn't been so simple as you'd think. . . . If the things my mother and father believed are true I shall only be delighted. But usually I can't believe it. No doubt if they knew this, my anti-clerical neighbours would forgive me. I shouldn't dream of telling them.'

'And you'll be satisfied to live in a village and grow lettuces?'

'My life can't possibly be simpler than it's been. Or poorer in the sorts of happiness men who are not professional soldiers think they deserve.'

'Do you resent your life?' Ward asked.

'Not for a moment.'

'Really?'

'Why should I?' Redon said simply. 'How many well-off soldiers do you imagine there are? . . . Yes. I resent one thing. It's wrong that even a soldier can spend his life doing what his government tells him to do without earning any respect.'

'Oh, come,' Ward protested. 'The French respect their army.'

'You're wrong. We're used when our particular virtues are needed. The rest of the time we're ignored. Or mishandled by the politicians.'

'Do you remember what you expected after the last war?'

'To prepare for the next,' Redon said. 'I remember ten years ago I went to Lorraine with my regiment, we were sent to form a guard of honour for Poincaré, he was going to dedicate a war memorial. . . . I've often wondered what a politician thinks when he makes a speech to a great many dead soldiers. I know what a general would think. Very much, I suppose, like an artist in front of a picture he finished so long ago that only his mind recognises it. Everything else in him, his nerves and his body, has forgotten it completely. . . . I was standing close to Poincaré, and I saw him for a long moment looking towards the east. He turned his back on the monument and said in a low voice: They'll come again. . . . That's what he was thinking in front of all the soldiers of the last war, those of us who were dead and those, like me, who were a little ashamed to be alive. But our crime isn't that we survived the war, it's our failure, inexcusable by the living and laughable to the dead, to prepare for this war. . . . You think that's immoral?'

'No.'

'You English are too sure of yourselves. You

expect never to be attacked. It's a kind of innocence and a kind of hypocrisy.'

'I can speak for two of us . . . the other was killed here, by the way, in the communication trench. We thought that after the war we should be living in a country where not a single tree had been cut down to make room for petrol pumps, and we expected to eat the same meals we ate in June 1914, with as much appetite, to wake with the same suddenness, to open the same books and walk about the streets where nothing would have changed, with all the happiness and stupidity of young men.'

'You're not stupid,' Redon said. 'You didn't expect anything of the sort.'

'No. I didn't. . . . But I spent years pretending to know what I wanted to do as a civilian. The pretence can be horribly boring. . . . I had the best of reasons for pretending: I married.'

Redon glanced quickly, almost without turning his head, at the table. 'Yes?'

Ward spoke partly to himself. 'Probably my wife would have forgiven my failures—I'm too quickly bored, I haven't enough friends—she refuses to count the half-dozen who were killed— I'm too anxious to avoid trouble, especially troublesome feelings—and my bad habits, telling

lies, biting my nails, impatience and the rest of
it.  But I'd had one success in my life, one
absolute success, and it was unforgivable.  I'd
been absorbed and happy during the war, too
happy, too absorbed; I'd used up a lifetime of
energy and enthusiasm, and my wife, poor girl,
knew she'd been cheated.'

'She was a stupid woman?'

'No, far from it.  She was clever, and as greedy
as any normal young woman.'

'A soldier ought not to marry.'

'I daresay.  But I wasn't a soldier,' Ward
said.

'The war taught you the need for friends and
removed them from you, it let you father a faith
on it and then killed it slowly before your eyes.
It asked you as though it were important for your
life and then, as though after all it had been
nothing much, not worth keeping, threw it back
on your hands.  Only an unusually polite woman
would have put up with you, still less thanked
you.'

'It was more than that.  You mayn't have
noticed it,' Ward said, 'but the world has just
shed a skin.  Men as well as women are less
satisfied and less hopeful, and less stupid.  It
takes more kindness than it did for them to live

together. . . . Besides, as soon as she'd got used to them my wife was bored by my looks; I was twenty-five when the war ended and I looked forty. . . . If it had been a less troublesome business I should have left her. . . . After a few years I began to expect another war and I waited for that.'

'Did a single other Englishman expect it?'

'Good God, yes. Thousands of them.'

'But you weren't ready.'

'Were you?' Ward said quickly.

'No. . . . You see why, when you hear my nephew and young Masson quarrelling. They bore me.'

'They'll be all right when you move off,' Ward said. 'They oughtn't to be shut up here.'

'You can see what political parties have done to the country,' Redon said.

'Oh, we have them in England,' Ward said. 'They don't give any trouble. In a serious crisis the leaders change sides. The balance—you've heard of our balance—straightens itself at once.'

'You have fewer illusions.'

'Evidently.'

'Or simpler minds,' Redon said.

'We're practically imbeciles.'

Redon smiled. 'A pity you didn't infect us.

It's too late now. There must have been a moment when Frenchmen started their habit of hating each other. Two thousand years ago some child was jealous of his brother and killed him, and by this time we're all descended from him. In a history of my province, written in the fourteenth century, every page ends with the phrase: After a long siege the town was taken and the men and women put to the sword. And it doesn't end there. When I was a child my grandfather showed me the courtyard where twelve hundred Protestants were executed while Catholic gentlemen and their wives looked on and clapped. And a third of the families in the village, a very small village, mark you, were wiped out during the Revolution. Always this frightful hatred between neighbours. This cruelty springing out of the earth itself, between Frenchman and Frenchman, between poor and rich, peasant and worker, left and right. In this war our young dead will find it easier to talk to their enemies. They will have fewer bitter things to say to each other.'

'You think so?'

'I know.'

'Tell me. What would you do, you, if it came to a civil war?'

'The only thing I could do,' Redon said. 'I should obey my orders.'

'Of course, but whose orders?'

'The general commanding for the Republic.'

'And if he ordered you to kill Frenchmen?'

'I should kill myself,' Redon said quietly.

'You could refuse.'

'I should only be shot. And rightly.'

'You would have set an example. If it was known, it might spread from a battalion to a division, from a division to a corps . . . and where's your civil war?'

'You talk like a civilian,' Redon said. 'I can't begin criticising my orders. If I refuse to obey an order so cruel that it sickens me, I may refuse the next because it will kill too many of my men. Hideous or not, the only thing I have to do is to obey. Where, in the middle of a war, can I draw a line between degrees of cruelty? Do you know? . . . I know how to obey without hesitating, it's the meaning of my life. If it fails me—it will fail if I'm ordered to kill Frenchmen—my only reason for existing will be wiped out, I shall be nothing. I shall be disgraced, I shall kill myself with less reluctance than I hand in an old rifle. And, believe me, with far less regret.'

'No, it's inhuman,' Ward exclaimed.

'War is inhuman,' Redon said.

'There's a point beyond which men can't be pushed without becoming monsters.'

Redon looked at him. 'Wasn't I a monster when I shot that boy in the back of the head just now?'

'It was necessary,' Ward said.

'Exactly,' Redon said sadly.

'There's justifiable and unjustifiable cruelty.'

'You mean there are cruel acts that advance the war, and others,' Redon said, 'just as cruel, which don't. How am I to know the difference between them? I'm not in charge of the war.'

'No, no, you're wrong. I can imagine a moment when I should know I had no human right to obey my orders. And I should refuse.'

Redon smiled. 'Ah, you're a mystic, after all. You have your inner light. One of God's Englishmen.'

'Pity everyone isn't.'

'My God, there would still be wars,' Redon said.

'They would be comparatively human.'

'You think that's a merit?'

'Unless there's any merit in being inhuman. . . . Tell me, how many times since this war started have you watched a man behaving better

G                    97

than he ever behaved in his life, enduring things, accepting his death, looking after his friend?'

'Hundreds,' Redon said. 'But that's not war. What do you think? War isn't its friendships, it's not even loyalty or courage or justice, it's forcing men to move when they're exhausted, and punishing the sleepiness of an eighteen-year-old sentry mercilessly and unjustly. And punishing your own failures more mercilessly, of course . . . if there is anything harder than ordering a boy to be shot . . . I ought not to say so, but I hate killing. Even an enemy. Just now when I was walking behind that German he hunched his shoulders forward like a child, like a schoolboy bending over his books . . . I had to shoot him then. . . . And if I were ordered to kill French boys . . .'

'Yes,' Ward said. 'Perhaps you ought to separate your young men. Why don't you send one of them off alone?'

'Which one?'

## 5

Lucien Vidal came quietly down the stairs. Redon looked at him kindly.

'What do you want, Lucien?'

'I want to talk to you,' Vidal said.

'Certainly.'

'Alone, please.'

'Do you want to talk about yourself?' Redon asked.

'It's partly personal.'

'Talk to both of us.'

'I'll go into the other cellar,' Ward said.

Redon looked at him. 'Oblige me by staying.'

'I can't go on,' Vidal said.

'What do you mean?'

'It's foolish to try to go on,' Vidal said. 'Where are we going?'

'You're going to find your regiment,' Redon said slowly, 'and stay with it, like other people.'

'No,' Vidal said, 'I can't.'

'What do you want to do?' Redon said, watching him. 'Hide here until you're caught and dragged out?'

'No.'

'Then what?'

'I can give myself up.'

'Do you know at all what you're saying?' Redon said, after a moment.

'Yes, of course,' Vidal said nervously. 'There's no reason why I shouldn't walk into Beaucourt and surrender to the German commander.'

Redon was silent.

'Well, is there?'

'I won't talk to you about your duty,' Redon said slowly. 'I'll remind you you're under orders.'

'Whose?'

'Mine, of course,' Redon said.

'You can't possibly take him with you,' Ward said. 'He's a liability.'

Redon ignored him. 'Will you tell me why you want to surrender?' he said.

'Simply because the war's lost,' Vidal said.

'Yes?' Redon said ironically. 'I suppose you have private news. Or is your intuition warning you?'

'It's not private,' Vidal said, 'and there is news.'

Ward looked at him. 'What is it?'

Vidal spoke triumphantly. 'Paris has been declared an open city, the Government has left.'

'Where did you hear this nonsense?' Redon said.

'Broussard's wireless is working again, the Englishman poked it. We heard part of the news bulletin. The truth this time.'

'Well?' Redon said. 'What difference can it make?'

'Why do you pretend not to know what it

means?' Vidal said. His voice rose. 'You know as well as I do. We could have seen it coming. What about the line of ambulances we saw smashed up by bombs and the one man crawling about among them like a fly? What about the people on the roads? What about our own breakdown, you saw the men give way, you weren't able to hold your own company, let alone the others. . . .'

Redon lifted his hand. 'What has any of this to do with you?'

'I refuse to get myself killed trying to reach an army which has been defeated,' Vidal said excitedly.

'A withdrawal isn't a defeat. We shall be fighting on the Loire.'

'Why not on the Pyrénées?' Vidal jerked his head at Ward. 'He doesn't believe you for a minute. He never did. He said, I heard him: The French won't stand. . . . His country is safe enough, the English won't ruin themselves, they'll cheat their way out.'

'I was talking about the Marne,' Ward said.

Redon moved his head. 'It's not in the least important. . . . Do you really know what you're doing?' he said to Vidal. 'Do you feel ill?'

'I'm perfectly sane, saner than you,' Vidal said.

'And you want to walk into Beaucourt, into a French village, where, if Broussard knows what he's talking about, there's only a German tank lieutenant and a few broken-down tanks . . . they're the enemy, they hold the place. . . .'

'As enemies, they're no worse than Masson,' Vidal interrupted. 'If I keep myself alive I can deal with him, but if I'm killed stupidly in this obstacle-race of yours . . .'

'You're indecent,' Redon said coldly, 'you and your private quarrels during a war.'

'This war was a mistake.'

Ward made an attempt to prick the balloon before it went up.

'My dear boy, so are all wars,' he said genially. 'Every war. Even one that ends in a crashing victory. The same result, happy or unhappy, could have been reached at a fraction of the cost, without killing a soul, not even a child. The difficulty begins when you try to persuade both sides they're going to lose and might as well give in at once. You could always persuade me of it, and probably both general staffs. But could you in your wildest moments hope to persuade the dear civilians who arrange wars, and declare them solemnly over the wireless, and make frequent speeches until the peace treaty is signed, and more and even more dishonest and stirring speeches when they unveil their monuments to the dead or encourage the survivors to enjoy being neglected? I haven't the least doubt France will be ruined by this war. And Germany and England and every other country of this vigorous Europe, so much more vigorous than America. Of course the war is a mistake. A bloody mistake. But you can't—you're unlucky—suddenly announce you're neutral. You should have run away before it started.'

'May I deal with this?', Redon said coldly. He turned to Vidal again. 'It's quite simple. You haven't been asked to decide whether this war is necessary or just, you've been asked to obey. Nothing else.'

'Very well, who am I obeying?' Vidal said. 'I can tell you. All those Jews and Jewish black-mailers who wanted a war.'

'Don't quote the newspapers to me,' Redon said. 'It disgusts me.'

Vidal made a gesture of despair, almost the gesture of a child.

'You're too old, I can't talk to you,' he said.

'Try,' Redon said gently.

'I know you're honest. The people who got us into this war counted on your honesty. They knew you would fight for them. But it's a horrible disaster! It must stop. It will be stopped. There are honest people who aren't ignorant. . . . Why did you shut me up when I was talking about the officer at Givet who surrendered to avoid attacking? He knew he was outnumbered and he had no tanks. . . .'

'A traitor I've never seen doesn't interest me. You, Lucien, are my nephew.'

'I'm not a traitor,' Vidal said bitterly. 'I'm only sick of this hopeless war.'

'Very well, I order you to go on,' Redon said. 'You'll give me your revolver, and you'll come with me, and Mr Masson, as if you were some little clerk or a shopkeeper we'd picked up.'

Vidal looked at him with hatred. 'I see. You'll shoot me in the back of the head, like that German.'

'You deserve it, but I shan't do it.'

'May I hear why?' Vidal said.

'There are limits to my strength,' Redon said slowly, 'and I would rather put your cowardice on my own bill.'

Ward tried again. 'Aren't we making too much of this?' he said. 'The commonsense way of taking it is that the boy's lost his nerve. Is there anything we can do to help him?'

'I value your advice, of course,' Redon said coldly and civilly. 'But principles are involved. . . .'

Ward threw his hands up. 'Oh, principles!'

'If your principles,' Vidal stammered, 'have tricked you into dying for the right of foreigners and Jews to ruin France, something is wrong with them. You can keep them, thank you. And your Jews.'

Redon looked at him. 'For the last time, Lucien. . . . You're like your mother when we were children, she was very gentle but she would let herself be whipped rather than change her mind. . . . You have the same forehead and eyes. . . . I ought to remind you of your father. . . . It's confusing. . . . He was a young man, he was less than a year older than you are. If he were alive he would be fighting, you can't be in any doubt what he would say to you.'

'The last war may have been necessary. I don't know—it was your war. This one is a mistake.'

Redon's voice changed. 'There's no mistake. You talk like a lawyer. I can't say worse. The simple unlawyerlike truth is that you came when you were ordered to defend the Republic—you couldn't get out of it—and now you're afraid.'

'Your Republic stinks, it's not worth defending,' Vidal said.

'Possibly you're right. I don't know and I'm not even remotely interested. I'm defending this farm, with its poor soil—and Broussard's sour wine and his cabbages and spiced bread.'

'The last war made them so safe, didn't it?' Vidal said.

'Oh, come, need we go into all that?' Ward said hurriedly. 'Technically, you ought to be shot as a deserter. But it would be ridiculous, as well as very unpleasant, if we began shooting each other. Here the four of us are—five, I was forgetting my young gib-cat—in this extremely tight corner. Are you prepared to desert your friends?'

'You're not my friends,' Vidal said.

Ward shrugged his shoulders.

'If you feel that——'

'One of you is English,' Vidal interrupted. 'You're both middle-aged. And I don't trust Masson. And—if you're talking of feeling—I feel nearer the German you killed.'

'Really?' Redon said quietly. 'You find points of sympathy with a youth who has been firing our villages and murdering helpless refugees?'

Vidal was on the point of breaking down. His voice rose.

'I tell you, the war did it.'

Yawning widely and shamelessly, Ward said, 'Let him go.'

'You can go,' Redon said.

Vidal swayed slightly. He did not answer.

'Before you go, you'll sit down and write a short statement,' Redon said.

'What about, for heaven's sake?' Ward asked.

'Write out what it is you're going to do,' Redon said. 'I shall put it in my pocket and keep it.'

'If you produce it after the war, he'll be shot,' Ward said. 'Why not at once?'

'I shan't produce it,' Redon said to Vidal quietly. 'I shall simply keep it, and you'll know it exists. You'll know it as long as you live. Go on, sit down and write it.'

The young man went over to the table and sat down. He looked at Redon.

'I used to be kept in myself, regularly,' Ward said to him.

'Have you your pen?' Redon asked.

'No, sir.'

Redon tore a page out of his notebook and put it with his pen on the table near Vidal. He turned away and spoke to Ward.

'I don't like to ask you to come upstairs, with your knee. But I want your advice and we can't talk where this fellow can hear us.'

'Oh, I daresay you're right,' Ward said. 'Give me a hand up the stairs, will you?'

He dragged himself up and limped to the foot of the stairs. It was obvious that his knee had become more painful. Redon helped him to climb the stairs.

6

Sitting with his back to them, Vidal listened without turning his head until they had gone. Then he drew the paper to him and began, slowly, to write. After a moment Pierre Masson came down the stairs. He crossed the room to the table, saw what Vidal was doing, and hesitated. He watched him for a moment.

'What are you writing? A poem?'

'Even if I were it has nothing to do with you,' Vidal said.

'Oh, I don't object to your poems.'

'Thanks.'

'I mean it,' Masson said.

Vidal looked up. 'You haven't read any.'

'Yes, the one in the *Revue de Paris*. You

described the Dordogne lying trapped by the hot sun, calmly expectant, a well-to-do councillor's wife in some town, Bergerac or Libourne, lying on her back waiting to be caressed by the warmth, by the movement of the lime-trees, by a word. It was charming.'

'You've forgotten one verse,' Vidal said softly. 'The lime-trees were hives of bees, an endless oppressive murmur. . . .'

'I'd forgotten . . .' Masson hesitated. 'I came to apologise for my bad temper. I insulted you.'

'I—it doesn't matter,' Vidal said.

Masson took no notice. 'To be honest I didn't like the shooting. He spoke to us on the way. He said in German: It will be another hot day. And you could feel it, although it was just light. The sky was very clear. When we turned into the road I thought: In one minute he'll be dead. Fifty seconds. Thirty. He moved his head a little. Perhaps he felt Redon lift his arm. There was a poplar he must have seen, one, rather a poor one. . . .'

'People do vile things, and excuse themselves because it's war,' Vidal said.

'Glorious things too. You don't know that Redon kept three hundred Germans out of a farm for twelve hours and brought half his men out alive. You were unlucky not to be with us. When he came in that morning we felt we'd won the war. If our line came unstitched there would always be Redon or someone else to knot it.'

'Much good his knots are. They didn't save Paris.'

'I ought to be able to understand you,' Masson said quietly. 'We're the same age and the same height. We're both long-sighted and I can't score off you by seeing a plane three seconds before you. We used the same school-books, we were provincials in Paris at the same time, but because you came from Beynac you shivered even in summer and I was always warm—a bit of luck, since I hadn't an overcoat.'

'Yes, I remember you at Buisson's lectures,' Vidal said. 'You stalked in as though you owned the place.'

'I was ashamed of being clumsy.'

'No one knew it,' Vidal said, with a half-smile. 'Why do you dislike me?'

Vidal hesitated. 'Your thick skull and hands. And you're an anarchist.'

'I? What nonsense!'

'Oh, I know you call yourself something equally stupid,' Vidal said. 'But you have the same wicked dreams. You pretend that men needn't be hungry or wifeless or childless or ignorant or unhappy. You take all the sense and dignity out of their lives and offer in its place what? A wireless set in every home. Horrible, horrible. And it's the best you can offer people you've robbed of their faith in God and the future.'

'The people I know haven't any future,' Masson said. 'Where could they find it in their poor fields? I was eight years old before I had a pair of shoes of my own.'

'If you'd had them you would still have been discontented.'

'I shouldn't have had corns,' Masson said.

'After this war you'll be poorer than ever.'

'I shall still be thankful I didn't miss it. I've never been happier, never liked people so much, or known what sleep meant, or cold or devotion. If, as you say, I dream about the future, I dream it at the other side of this war, and in the same shapes.'

'God knows how many thousands of Frenchmen will be killed before you wake up,' Vidal said.

Masson smiled shyly. 'Don't let's begin quarrelling. We can agree on being Frenchmen.'

'Not even that,' Vidal said.

'Why not?'

'Shall I tell you how I see France? A young

woman, the wife of a ploughman or fisherman, with a wide throat and red hands, simple-minded, devout, gay. She has children already, and she'll never know unless you tell her that she's poor and ignorant.'

'A pity we didn't live in one of those intervals when nothing happens except earthquakes and famines,' Masson said. 'The only thing I really wanted to do was to watch birds, at home I used to sleep in the ditch to keep an eye on a family of magpies. Even this morning I kept my eyes open for a hawk. . . . You would have written charming poetry. You'd have joined a reactionary party, of course, but without doing much harm. Even now if you get a chance to write, the future will forgive you your poisonous ideas. It won't care how selfish, how reactionary you were, it will read your words and love you for them. No one will remember what I do.'

'I may be killed in this war of yours.'

'It isn't mine.'

Vidal raised his voice. 'You wanted to fight Hitler. If we'd left him the rest of Europe he would never have touched France.'

'D'you suppose fear and treachery could have been confiscated at the frontier?' Masson said.

'Why not?'

'The air on both sides is the same. We couldn't breathe freely here while men were being choked to death over there.'

'And when we're both killed, I with my poems not written down, and you without knowing anything about herons—you don't have them in the Ardennes—what use will it be?'

'Other men will live better lives,' Masson said.

'How do I know that? It doesn't look like it. Did you ever imagine yourself shooting an unarmed man in the back?'

'No.'

'Ah,' Vidal said. 'You feel guilty.'

'It's for the future. Any brutality now . . . any guilt . . . I—you—have to accept it.'

'I won't.'

'You can't help it,' Masson said slowly.

'I'm turning my back.'

'What d'you mean?'

'There's no hope in tolerating people like you,' Vidal said. 'None. Twenty years ago we defeated the Germans, since then they've hated us and we've feared them. Now they're defeating us; we live at the ends of a balance, first one and then the other dips head down into a gulf of shame, misery, defeat. . . . It's unbearable. The people who have been ruling us and making money and cheating, and their clever mean hopes, are unbearable. Like the horrible unmentionable deaths. . . . They broadcast a lot of things, why don't they broadcast the screams of a boy trying to be quiet? How long do you suppose even the politicians could listen?'

'They'd switch off.'

'Yes, they'd switch off. They do it every day. . . . I want to stop such sounds coming from French mouths. And German ones. . . . I want to break the current joining evil done to evil suffered. Let it break now! Let's silence the elderly politicians. Let's cut down to the lies and cut them out mercilessly, with the Jews who live on us. We shall be poor and weak for a long time. But with bread grown in our own soil, and wine. . . . A France our great poets would know if they came back to it.'

Masson had listened with a sharply watchful air. 'Yes, very fine. What are you going to do?'

'Why should I tell you?' Vidal said.

'Don't, if you're ashamed.'

'I'm not coming with you,' Vidal said.

'Oh?'

'We're cut off here. I'm sick of this madness. I'm going into Beaucourt to surrender to the first German I see on the road.'

'You're a coward,' Masson said quietly and bitterly. 'I knew you were.'

'Just as you like,' Vidal said. He shrugged his shoulders. He was trembling.

'I shan't let you do it,' Masson said.

'Try. You're not my superior officer.'

'Are you saying that Captain Redon said you could go?' Masson said. 'I don't believe you.'

'No? Ask him.'

'He doesn't know you, he's too old,' Masson said coldly, 'he imagines you can be trusted. I know what you're doing, and I shan't let you leave here. You poet!'

'Go and catch birds.'

'You know the way Redon's going,' Masson said. 'You'll set your German friends on us.'

Vidal was shocked. 'You have a good memory,' he said, stammering and angry.

'Yes, I remember you probably saved my life at Avesnes,' Masson said in a low voice. 'They'll make you talk.'

'Get out of my way,' Vidal said.

Masson snatched his revolver and got between Vidal and the stairs.

'No, you don't.'

Vidal threw himself on Masson. They struggled for a minute, and Vidal was pushed back until he managed to twist Masson's hand with the revolver. When it went off Masson was shot and staggered slowly backward. Vidal backed out of his way, looking at him with horror. Masson reached the table and leaned against it.

'You did that with your left hand,' he said. 'Clever of you.'

### 7

Before Vidal could move, Murray ran noisily down the stairs.

'What's happened?' he said.

'I've hurt myself,' Masson said. It was difficult for him to speak.

'You were here, Lucien,' Murray said quickly. 'What happened?'

'We quarrelled . . .' Vidal began.

'No,' Masson said, with an effort of will. 'I thought the thing was empty. Never mind.'

'Go and get someone,' Murray said.

Vidal went quickly away, without looking back. Masson had slid down by the table on to the floor. The English boy ran to the blanket rolled up against the wall, shook it out, and pushed a fold of it under Masson's head. Masson drew his knees up and turned over like a child, pressing his face into the blanket. Major Ward came downstairs slowly and painfully. He bent over Masson, lifted his head slightly, then laid it down and looked briefly, without touching it, at his side. He straightened himself and looked round.

'Where's the other one?'

'I should think he's cleared off,' Murray said.

'These Frenchmen . . .' Ward said. 'They'll make a nuisance of themselves on the Last Day. . . . You'd better straighten him out.'

Redon came in as he said it.

# CHAPTER III

## I

THE cellar was empty and in darkness, the shutters closed. Closed against an evening which belonged to the Germans, and to presages of defeat. The French who had stayed in the villages or in farms off the roads shut themselves early into their houses, before dark, to avoid any risk of being questioned and perhaps, since the Germans here were not sure of themselves yet, shot. By the same precaution they avoided the hour between dusk and night when an older woman, or two or three of the older women, used to walk out past the new schoolhouse and the memorial, cross the footbridge over the stream that runs into the Ancre, and follow the road out beyond the fields to the field of immortals, to the war cemetery. It was not one of the better-kept cemeteries— small, and with a breach in the wall over which children and goats could step. No one had been near it for days, they were ashamed to look at it and they were ashamed of its shabbiness. Better if we had looked after it ourselves, some of them

thought; if we had known who was coming to
see it we would have.

On the cellar pressed the weight of a day during
which the Germans had crossed another French
river, the Seine.

Martine came down the steps. She was carrying a candle, and sheltered the flame with her hand
until she had set it on the table. Then she lit the
lamp and looked round. She folded up a blanket
lying in a heap on the floor, and made a show of
dusting table and chairs. Murray came out of the
cellar on the left, yawning and stretching his arms.

'Martine,' he said. He was startled.

'Yes? Did you want me?' she said.

'No, I hadn't heard you, that's all.'

'I'm just going.'

'What time is it? My watch has stopped.' It
was the truth this time.

'I don't know. I think—about nine o'clock,'
Martine said.

He watched her. 'Do you ever do nothing?'

'Why should I?' she said, smiling.

'If you were an English girl,' Murray said,
'you'd go to the village dances and you'd go in
by bus twice a week to the pictures. The other
evenings you'd put your best frock on and walk
about.'

'We always have a dance on July the four-teenth.'

'You won't tonight,' Murray said.

'No. . . . My friend used to come for me. Bertha. She was born the same day as me, she's a little taller. She can see across fields in the dark. To be even with her I used to pretend to hear everything.'

'Where is she?' Murray asked.

'I don't know, her family went with the others. She hadn't even time to tell me they were going. . . . You spoke of walking. We always walked to Beaucourt on Sunday evening. Just where the road turns you see the lights of the houses suddenly, like a surprise. Bertha said: They promise something.'

'It was nothing very pleasant if it was this.'

'We shan't always be at war,' Martine said lightly, 'the Germans will go. They always have done.'

Murray smiled at her. 'Your friend didn't see far enough in the dark. She could have told us what to expect tomorrow or the next day.'

'At this time . . . you'll be walking across a field.'

'I'm afraid so,' Murray said. 'Walking doesn't amuse me.'

'Not at night? We used to come home in summer with bare feet, we crossed the stream and kept on the grass at the side. Would an English girl like doing that?'

'I doubt it.'

'Oh.'

'Don't you mind being alone?' Murray asked.

'Yes. . . . I can see the roofs of the village from my room. I know what the house is like under some of them. The stairs turn right, I say, the cupboard opens under the stairs, the bedroom door opens inward, and the bed is set north and south, or east and west. It should be north and south if you want to sleep properly.'

'Very well,' Murray said lightly, 'tomorrow morning when you get up——I know you get up with the light——I shall be going to sleep in a ditch running north and south, and if I can't find one in time and I'm caught . . .'

'You won't be caught.'

'Don't pretend now that you can see at night.'

'Why should you be?'

'Because these things happen,' Murray said. 'Aren't you caught here, in your farm, in your bedroom with the coloured photograph of Dieppe——?'

'Rouen.'

'Any place you've never seen. I'll come back after the war, with my mother: we'll take you to see Rouen.'

'When do you start?' she asked.

'About ten.' He frowned. 'I don't like going off without him, it's a bad thing to do.'

'Your officer? But he'll be safe. He's much cleverer than you are.'

'I know,' Murray said. 'He thinks so.'

2

Captain Redon came down the stairs and walked straight to the table, ignoring them. Martine drew back quickly. She looked at the young Englishman with a guilty ironical smile, and hurried away.

'Is there any news?' Murray asked.

'The Germans entered Paris this morning,' Redon said without looking at him.

'Is it much damaged?'

'It wasn't defended,' Redon said.

Murray flushed. 'I'd forgotten. . . . I'm glad it hasn't been knocked about. I wonder if we shall defend London. I hope so.'

'Your Government will decide that for you.'

Murray reminded himself that he was talking to a superior officer. 'I'll go, sir, if you have nothing for me to do here,' he said.

'Go.'

Murray took the candle from the table and went off with it into the cellar on the left. Left alone, Redon bent over the table and began to draw on it with a wide movement of his arm. Major Ward was making his painful descent of the staircase. Redon went across to help him.

'Thanks,' Ward said.

He limped over to the table and sat down in his usual place with his back to the shaft.

'You were right,' Redon said. 'But if we had defended Paris it would have changed everything. We should have held on to what remained. . . . With the knot of Paris cut, the whole line is coming unstitched. Why? What has happened to us?'

'You were out-tanked, out-generalled—and out-hearted.'

'What do you mean?'

'The Germans knew they would win. Your men were merely brave or merely fatalist. You were always saying: We must finish it. It sounded resolute, and what you meant was: We can never face this again. Men who have stiffened their muscles only to hold on can hold until they're killed. Then the enemy steps over them. If they have bad generals they don't even hold, they lose heart.'

'Did the English think they would win?' Redon said.

'Your troops are tough and very brave,' Ward said quickly. 'They're badly led.'

'I worded my question badly,' Redon said.

'Oh, we're no better prepared for this war than you. But if you leave us to go on alone we shall give an excellent account of ourselves. It's a long time since an enemy landed in England. Eight hundred years. We feel safe. Like you we have our symbols, but none of them will turn round at a critical moment and destroy us. Be honest, Redon. Admit you were stunned when you knew the Marne had gone.'

'The Marne, like the Aisne and the Somme, is a nerve of France.'

'Your nerves must be as much English as French,' Ward said. 'The edges of the Aisne, the Marne and the Somme are contours of our lives, too. You couldn't touch the smallest field there without laying a hand on us, on the dust of endurance and gaiety we left with our bodies at the roots of your grass.'

'We passed a French war cemetery,' Redon said, 'on the way here—the last German war, you understand—it had been ploughed up by bombs. The assault on it of two German airmen. They dive-bombed it until it was ruined, more ruined than a village. It may not seem important. . . . I don't say that the dead suffered in any way, they'd paid that when they were alive—when they were cold, when they were wounded. They'd already felt all that civilians in this war feel when German airmen come down to machine-gun them in the fields and roads. But when I saw it I knew the Germans would lose: in the end they'll be defeated and punished not for anything they've done to children who were alive and happy a month ago—for their cruelty to the dead, for a callousness that goes past those who are living and may strike back, and crushes those who can't defend themselves now. Or so those two think. They're mistaken.'

'I daresay,' Ward said. 'Though it's always possible the dead have quite different notions of justice. . . . Probably you're right. . . . Later on someone will be forced to avenge the Germans you've punished. Oh, justly. I admit the justice.'

'We can leave that to the future to arrange and settle.'

'It's possible the future will speak any language except French or German. . . . Or English for that matter.'

'So long as it doesn't speak German,' Redon said.

'Oh, if we're talking about their habits. . . . Energetic bores. . . . But what are we going to do with them?'

'The sensible thing would be to kill the lot. They keep war alive in Europe. Five Prussian wars in eighty years. It's too much.'

'Impossible,' Ward said. 'One of them would escape and the whole thing begin again. A pity. . . . But imagine yourself living afterwards with a woman and children of your own.'

'We could do it if it were any use. We could tell lies about it. We could hold our tongues. What would our women have to complain of? They would be able to look at their children without anguish. And if their husbands disliked talking to them about the war, that's not unusual. Did you find it easy to talk to your wife about the last war, or to any non-combatant or neutral?'

'No,' Ward said. He had been examining the table and the lines Redon had scrawled on it. 'Why were you drawing a map of France?'

'To prove it's still possible to defeat the

Germans——if the High Command seriously wants
to.'

'Why shouldn't it?'

'Who am I to fathom the minds of the General
Staff?' Redon said softly. 'An infantry captain.
Too old to be promoted.'

Ward traced his finger up and across the map.
'Is this the Loire?'

'Yes.'

'I'd forgotten how it curved. The arc of a
bow.'

'And the Rhône as straight as an arrow. . . .
Our armies could stand on the Loire.'

'Another symbol?' Ward said, smiling.

'So you think we're defeated?'

'I think you'll surrender. It's not quite the
same thing.'

'Obviously not.'

'France is an old, highly civilised country——'
Ward began.

Redon interrupted him. 'No older than the
Germans.'

'But humanised. All the marks of a civilisation at its highest point are scrawled across it,
your vineyards, bookshops, the workrooms of
your artists, sculptors, chefs, wheelwrights, dyers,
silk-weavers. You have no great musicians,

only civilised ones. Since the Middle Ages, all the most powerful ideas have been born here. Your civilisation has tougher roots than German savagery, but you've retreated before them and you're going to give in. Why? Because the only passion millions of Frenchmen have in common is fear. . . . It's always easy to suspect someone in your own family of trying to cheat you out of your money. You hate with ideas, too —that's always cruel. And you hadn't children.'

'D'you know how many millions of young Frenchmen died in the last war?' Redon said.

'Why didn't you replace them?'

'We replaced some of them. Was it a success? We've already lost some of our replacements, two or three of them died in my arms, with the foolish or frightened look of very young soldiers who don't know the ropes yet. If the country is better off for these young deaths I've nothing to say. But why have I escaped, and boys who never killed anyone have been killed? Obviously war, whatever it is, isn't justice. . . .'

'So you're one of those who want to give in now?' Ward said.

'No.'

'What would you do—if you could do anything?'

'I should speak to Marshal Pétain,' Redon said slowly.

'Do you know him?'

'No. I saw him once. It was at Verdun—after it had been cleared of Germans at the end of that long bloody defence. It was at night. I'd come out of my cellar to breathe, you couldn't call it fresh air, the smell of the thousands of murdered bodies, French and German, was still too strong. I was standing in the darkness, thinking, but without any feeling of relief, of the hell we had escaped. A few of us. At certain moments you reach a depth of fatigue when death would only be the relaxing of a nerve, stretched against the intolerable for too long. I'd reached that moment, it even occurred to me that I'd been dead when I stepped out of the tunnel, I could feel so little difference between my shoulder and the wall I was leaning against. . . . A man came towards me, slowly, he was walking as though his feet were catching in the earth and furrows. He halted in front of me and I saw him, he was the man whose Order of the Day— Be brave, we shall defeat them—had stiffened us to hold out. He spoke to me and I looked at him. For all my respect, my reverence, I had nothing to say to him. He was going on, but he turned

I

back. You've been here all the time? he said
to me. I found my voice and said: Yes, General.
His face altered. The eyes, he has very clear eyes,
went away from me into some other place and
he looked over my head towards the mound.
After a moment he said: Is there anything you
want? No, General, I said. He lifted both his
hands, small hands for a man like that. No,
what could you want, what could any man want,
he said, who has lived through that? Then
before I could think of an answer—if there had
been an answer—he said: If I'd realised the cost
I wouldn't have had it defended. It was not
worth it. . . . And he walked away, leaving me to
reflect that a general who knows too much is
worse perhaps than one who knows too little.
Less use. I believe that if Pétain saw Tours,
Bordeaux, Marseilles, and all the villages and
obscure towns of France threatened with the
fate of Verdun, he would give in at once.'

'Surely he would be right?' Ward said.

'No. . . . The country must be defended—
even if it costs every life and every village.'

'And afterwards? What would France be
without Frenchmen and French villages?'

Redon said, 'The country of her last days and
of all her days. The country of Montaigne and

Pasteur, and the country of all her peasants and soldiers.'

'The world would forget them.'

'The world hasn't forgotten Greece,' Redon said.

Ward struck the table. 'No, no, if you gave them the choice most people would prefer to live. . . . Besides, war has become horrible. In the last war you could still think about the enemy with respect and sympathy, even at Verdun.'

'At Verdun especially.'

'But no one,' Ward said, 'who's seen a village destroyed from the air, ripped open, its children broken with their toys, and the bodies of its women, can think of the destroyers except with horror.'

'With pity and no forgiveness,' Redon said slowly. 'It comes of debasing armies with politics. As soon as they're told to fight for an idea men become brutal.'

'Or quarrel among themselves.'

Redon pressed his hands together. 'Or as you say, they quarrel and kill each other.'

There was a moment's silence.

'Why did you go to the front?' Ward said. 'You could have stayed at the base.'

Redon laughed. 'So that nobody could

131

mistake me for anyone but a soldier who hasn't managed to get himself promoted. Why did you come back?'

'Not as a soldier.'

'What?'

'I began to write after the last war. It has taken me twenty years to learn to write so coldly that no one could mistake what I meant. It's a recipe for failing as a writer.'

'Good. We're both failures,' Redon said gaily.

'When this war started—at last—it was obviously a war to allow writers to write what we please. So I rejoined.'

'Yes, of course,' Redon said politely. 'What was your real reason?'

Ward lifted his hand and let it fall on the table. 'A foolish, immoderate liking for war. . . . Oh, not for war. For all the things that according to you aren't war. The battalion moving up at night. Minutes spent writing orders in places that were all very like this cellar. An hour or two of unusual happiness, hours without any past or future, not run off like ordinary minutes . . . you lived in them as you would live if you were ten times more sensitive and alert. . . . The few minutes in the early morning when the area

132

in front of the trench was becoming visible, and
what at night was menacing, and dull or pitiless
in daylight, suddenly and for a very short time
was an image—such as my poor brain could
read—an image of infinity. . . . No, you're right,
I didn't come back for any sober reason—though
I could find plenty.'

'Well?'

'I came because I was fascinated by war.'

'Yes,' Redon said.

'You think I'm a fool.'

'I think you were deceiving yourself.'

'Why not?'

'Yes, why not?' Redon said. 'You wouldn't
call this part of the country handsome, would
you? But I caught myself looking at it the other
evening with actual astonishment. We'd been
retreating all day, I was half dead, my face was
stiff with dust and sweat, I leaned against the
wall of a house with a field in front of it and a
miserable stream. There was one poplar. I'd
closed my eyes and when I opened them I saw
the whole of France in this poor field, all its
rivers, the Loire, all its forests in a single half-
grown tree, and all its ordinary soldiers in my
servant, who'd been wounded and was trying to
find something in my haversack with his sound

arm. It was probably fatigue, but it was moving, and it was the war that had given it to me.'

'Damned if I've enjoyed this war,' Ward said abruptly.

Redon smiled. 'Not at all?'

'I don't know whether it's age. Or only the idea of its going on and on until the whole of England and Europe looks like this corner of France. But it hasn't been the same. I know better what to do now and I do it less willingly. And without any pleasure.'

'Because you expected something you had no right to expect the war to give you. An intense life. . . .'

'I had it last time,' Ward said.

'You were a young man.'

'So war is only fit for young men. And they either die of it or grow old.'

'Or,' Redon said, 'they begin to accept it.'

'Do you?'

'Accept it? Obviously.'

Ward leaned forward. 'Why? Tell me why.'

'It's simple. . . . I have never believed that men are naturally brave, truthful and obliging. Perhaps you do. In that case you can't accept war. Why should you? It kills people who only asked to be allowed to live. And have children. And

134

find the right answers to problems. And enjoy
the light. And eat. And drink. . . . And dis-
tinguish light from dark.'

'Why shouldn't we live? Simply live. I
haven't a natural enemy in the world. Except
myself.'

'Perhaps you kill yourself when you kill
Germans,' Redon said.

'Simple things, food, rest and work. Aren't
they? We could see to it that no one goes short
of them.'

'Then arrange at the same time for courage
and self-sacrifice to come through with our
second teeth,' Redon said. 'Or they'll always
be in danger of vanishing. . . . They can die
out. . . . Men don't behave well without trying.
If Hitler wins he'll tear up the growth of honesty
and gentleness among us by the roots, children
will be praised for spying on their parents, poets
and scientists will be rewarded for lies, human
love and freedom and pity will be killed.'

'Only for a time. Perhaps for hundreds of
years.'

'No, they might be destroyed,' Redon said
quietly. 'Men might stop trying to be human.
Suppose we begin thinking that our lives are
more important than decency and mercy—I don't

insist on freedom. . . . Suppose we believers in truth and gentleness refuse duty. . . . Does it matter in the least how many imperfect little lives are lost in defence of them? Suppose the only way we can defend them is by dying? . . . Infinitely simpler, believe me, than arranging for men to be perfect.'

'No one enlists with the idea of dying,' Ward said. 'Like you, like any ordinary man, I enlisted to kill.'

'Obviously. Why not? You agreed that decency and the rest must be defended. And you kill.'

'It's still horrible,' Ward said.

'Yes. And you're willing to go on.'

'For the same reason as you. I prefer to die free.'

'That's not my reason,' Redon said. 'I prefer dying as an ordinary Frenchman.'

'Probably it's the same thing,' Ward said, smiling.

'Civil of you.'

'You've been let down by your politicians,' Ward said.

'Not by our ordinary soldiers. . . .'

'Certainly not.'

'I'll tell you something. The morning of May

twelfth I was near an airfield where I knew the
Group Commander, an old friend, and I walked
up to call on him. I wish you'd known him.
He was severe and stubborn, as merciless with
others as with himself. I'd left my battalion
three days before, it was still in the line near
Sedan and I knew what it was going through.
They were being slaughtered by the German
airmen like cattle, or like refugees. We used
to watch the sky for any glimpse of a French
plane. Not one. The Germans came out of
the sun like wasps. . . . My friend excused himself calmly, he hadn't a single machine fit to send
up in daylight. Hundreds of day-flying planes,
with their pilots, were being kept uselessly in
the south of France, he'd been refused when he
begged for one squadron, and yet a message had
come through from headquarters, that morning,
ordering him to send a night-bombing squadron
over Sedan at once. Why, I said to him, since
it's useless? Merely to give the infantry the
illusion of being supported. You know how
much, in actual war, depends on illusions. . . .
He re-wrote the order, to give it the right brevity
for men who are going to be killed. The pilots
themselves had no illusions. Their old Amyots,
good enough to be taken up at night, have a top

speed of two hundred kilometres. They were useless against Messerschmitts flying at four hundred. They would be wiped out of the sky, and when I watched a section getting ready I felt uneasy. . . . Perhaps the cost of illusions is higher in this war than in previous ones. Too high. Or I notice it more. . . . The crew of one of the Amyots were grumbling in front of the Group Commander, as openly as though he'd praised one of them at last. I couldn't stop myself saying: What use is it to kill these men, the others in the trenches will die anyhow? He didn't answer, he pushed past me and ordered the rear-gunner out of the machine. . . . Clear out, you, I want your seat. . . . You know, he was happily married, he had children and a charming house. On the Loire, too. . . . He turned and looked at me and roared with laughter. Five years without hearing from you, he said, and you have the face to walk in just as I'm going to Berlin with five other stiffs. . . . The squadron had never heard him make a joke, and they were still smiling when they took off, and in two hours five out of the six machines were down in flames and my friend was dead. . . . If you're thinking of Sedan, a futile death. But if you think of the future—France defeated—I know why he did it.

To be remembered. . . . He was fortunate. . . .
He counted on someone taking the tale back to
his village. At any rate the schoolboys will hear
it, and our next victory will happen a generation
sooner. . . . As soon as the next fat man, my nurse
used to say.'

'I'll take your word for the fat man,' Ward
said.

Redon smiled. 'Thanks.'

'Poor devils all the same,' Ward said.

'What?'

'The children you've just sent up for another
war.'

'My dear fellow, they'll do it all right,' Redon
said.

He had begun buttoning up his collar, and he
took his haversack from the shelf, and looked
in it.

Ward looked at him. 'You off now?'

'Yes.'

'Will you do me a kindness?'

'What d'you want?' Redon said. 'My pen?
Torch?'

'Neither, thanks.' Ward hesitated. 'I wish
you'd take young Murray with you. He's
certain to lose himself.'

'What are you going to do?'

Ward spoke in a low voice. 'Between ourselves, my knee's worse. The best thing I can do is crawl out and get as far from the farm as possible.'

'I see.'

'I'd like the boy to get away first,' Ward said.

'You'd better send him by himself,' Redon said after a moment.

'Just as you please,' Ward said.

'He'll be safer alone.'

'I daresay,' Ward said stiffly.

'I must get off.'

Ward scarcely glanced at him. 'Right. . . . Goodbye.'

Redon hesitated. Then, with a slight smile and a glance over his uniform, he went.


### 3

Ward was alone for a minute.

'So much for our ally,' he said aloud.

He pulled himself up and took a few painful steps towards the staircase, hesitated, and went back to the table. He bent over the map again, and laughed.

'The Loire!'

Richard Murray came in from the other cellar, blowing out his candle in the doorway. He watched Ward drag himself round the table to his usual seat.

'Did I hear Captain Redon going, sir?'

'You did.'

'I take it he's gone for good.'

'Yes, he's gone,' Ward said. 'No more allies. Thank God. We can set about winning the war.'

The hatch that had been lowered gently by Redon was flung noisily up and Broussard came downstairs with his usual deliberation. The Englishmen watched him.

'Evening, Broussard,' said Ward. 'We shall be out of here in half an hour.'

'Please yourself,' Broussard said. 'The Boches will be here in an hour or so.'

'Do you know that?' Ward said sharply.

'A corporal and a couple of men were on their way here when I was in the field. From Beaucourt. They said they were requisitioning the farm and gave me two hours to clear out. . . .The war must be over.'

'And why?'

'They were civil,' Broussard said. 'They warned me not to take anything with me, of course. And I handed over the money in my pocket. But that's a matter of form. Civil or not, they're Boches.'

Martine had come almost silently downstairs. He looked at her.

'Are you ready, my girl?'

'Yes,' Martine said.

She moved back so that she could see Murray. The two of them stood and looked at each other across the table without speaking or trying to move closer together.

'Where are you going?' Ward said.

'St Quentin.'

'And why in heaven's name go there?'

'Because the war's finished there,' Broussard said. 'Whatever's been done to it is done.'

'In a week or two it will be finished in France. You'll be able to go where you like.'

'Perhaps. That won't give me my farm back. I re-made it, you can see for yourself I re-made it, out of barbed wire and mud. Next year I should have married the girl off and let some young man in on a good thing. In an hour the Boches will move in here and that's the end of France. This time they'll stop. They've been yelling for living room long enough.'

'You'll get it back,' Ward said.

'Perhaps.' Broussard shook himself gently. 'At least my God they didn't simply take over. We should have been shot. Stupid, eh? We've had enough of it here!'

Ward looked at him casually.

'Why did you keep me here, Broussard?'

'I don't do things for nothing,' Broussard said, grinning. 'I assure you. Last war a sergeant of your lot saved my life, and lost an arm. I owed you his arm. Our family is known for paying its bills. . . . Well, I can feel the rifle in my backside. . . . If you try to get through I advise going south-west. . . . They say our Government of heroes is at Tours. You'll find a few clothes you can take, and drop your uniform somewhere. Not here. How's your knee?'

'Not so good.'

'You should give yourself up.'

'I'll think about it,' Ward said.

'You have a lot of time. Come, Martine.'

He went off. Martine followed him, and Ward turned his head to watch her. Murray spoke for the first time.

'Hope you'll be all right,' he said in a light voice.

She shook her head, half smiling. Murray turned away. She looked back from the doorway, but already he had his back to her. Ward was tearing up gently the letter he had been writing.

4

'Now, my boy, off you go,' he said.

'Where to?' Murray said, smiling.

'How well do you know the country?'

'I've spent several holidays in Paris,' Murray said. 'I know my way about.'

'Good. You'll be able to avoid running into Boches in the Champs Élysées. What else?'

'I suppose they really would have destroyed Paris if the French had defended it,' Murray said.

Ward dragged himself and his chair round to the left side of the table and began to work over Redon's map.

'Why not?' he said, bent over the map. 'Why should they spare it? They want to win the war and they enjoy destruction. . . . It was a German who explained that they're driven to possess other countries brutally, because they're not loved. What a lot those children who tempt airmen to machine-gun them have to answer for!'

'But why love?' Murray said with energy.

'Why aren't they satisfied with their own lives?
Do I run about asking to be loved? Do the
French? Why is it only Germany that flings
itself into these paroxysms of affection for other
people's goods, and rolls about Europe smashing
and killing and stealing, when it isn't asking to
be admired for its strength?' His voice cracked
with a sudden fury and hatred. 'If you ask me,
since we can't be expected to spend the rest of
our lives flattering the Germans, we ought to
scatter them over the face of the earth and live
quietly.'

Ward looked up. 'Probably. . . . Just take a
look at this map, will you? Here's where we
are, this is the Ancre, here's Albert, this is the
Somme. You see the way the rivers lie across
France—he didn't trouble to put in the Seine,
I suppose he'd given it up for lost—except the
Saône and the Rhône, which run handsomely
north and south, through the most charming
country in the world. Bar none. Now, if
you——'

'Pity. I never was much good at maps,'
Murray said.

'Attend, please,' Ward said sharply. 'You'd
better make your way south-east at first. Let me
see, now. . . .'

'I'm not going,' Murray said.

'What did you say?'

'Not without you,' Murray said pleasantly.

'Don't waste my time,' Ward said.

'We only can move at night. Your knee will slow us down, but what does it matter? We're not postmen.'

'Thank you, I haven't the faintest intention of allowing you to be heroic at my expense,' Ward said. 'It wouldn't amuse me at all to have you crawling about at my heels.'

'Sorry. But I'm not going.'

Ward frowned. 'You're under my orders.'

'A fat lot of good that does you,' Murray said mildly. 'It takes three to make a court-martial.'

'Damn you,' Ward said. 'I don't want you hanging about. I can manage better alone.'

'I see. Pure self-interest. You're going to let me crash about among these charming rivers by myself.'

'My dear fellow, we have no time to argue. Off you go, pick up some of Broussard's clothes, and clear out. Find your own way, since you're incapable of listening to instructions. As soon as you've gone, I shall stroll off myself.'

'I watched your strolling method just now,' Murray said in his young quiet voice.

'What?'

'Your leg is out of commission.'

'I can move at my own pace all right,' Ward said.

'You don't mean to try. . . . I wish you'd tell me how many shots you have left.'

'What? Three.'

'Let's say two Germans, or two and a half. With luck.'

'Have it your own way,' Ward said. 'You're a pretty good bore. . . . I'm going to sit over there and pot at Germans as they come down the steps.'

'We shall do much better one on each side of the steps.'

'Listen. In a show of this sort,' Ward said carefully, 'it's always a little difficult to decide between your feelings and your duty. You have all the proper feelings for your age, but your duty obviously is to get back to England. The French are knocked out. In a week or two we shall be fighting the little Boche alone. We shall beat him, of course. We know more about warfare than any other people, Germans included, and you ought to be there giving a hand. . . . Don't look at me in that way, I'm not a high-minded patriot, it's simply a question of where you're most needed.'

'What's my chance of getting through, sir?'

'Excellent.'

'What's my chance of getting through?' Murray repeated.

Ward hesitated. 'Perhaps one in a hundred.'

Murray laughed. 'At that price I'm the best judge of my duty. I shall stay here and kill Germans. My widow's mite. All the more to my credit since I'm naturally peaceful. I fired at a fellow in Arras but he didn't seem to mind.'

'If I had your sound knee I should go. I assure you.'

'We all have our theories,' Murray said cheerfully. 'Besides, you know your way. We should have had a chance.'

Ward's face twitched. 'If only that cautious ally of ours had taken you with him.'

'Do you mean to say you asked him?'

'I did. He said you'd be safer alone.' Ward jerked himself straight suddenly in his chair. 'My God, what a fool I am,' he said. 'A dumb fool.'

'What?'

'He wasn't thinking of getting away, he was deciding how to get himself killed off.'

'More heroics,' Murray said, smiling.

'He had so little to say about poor Masson I

took it he was indifferent. . . . He wants to get out before the French turn on each other. I know them. Justice, national rebirth and the rest will keep their proper size in France, hard, narrow, sharp. They'll kill like lawyers.'

'I don't see what we can do about it,' Murray said.

'I could have been polite.'

'Well, he's gone.'

'Yes. . . .' Ward said nothing for a minute. He spoke quietly. 'I ask you—I'm not ordering you, I'm asking you to go.'

'Sorry, and all that.'

'This isn't much of a Verdun, you know.'

'It's the first I've struck,' Murray said.

Ward sighed. 'Right. We'll stay.'

There was a short silence.

'Funny it should be us,' Murray said lightly. 'You here in 1916 and me from the new lot.'

'You haven't our illusions,' Ward said.

'Does it matter?'

'Yes, I think so. If this was October 1916, if Jamie was standing there, he'd be able to think—it was the kind of thing he would think, he was a farmer as well as a poet—that in England at any rate no war would be able to foul woods and blast villages and streets out of memory.'

'It's a fatuous game,' Murray said. 'Why do we do it?'

'You know as much as I do.'

Murray smiled. 'They say it's a judgement. The world is sick and must die. Pity about the children.'

'They say anything. It's just as likely to be something you can't get rid of. There are always barbarians. And they come back. The Romans push them across the Rhine and the Danube this year, next year, some time. Never. Rome holds out, then it falls. France held out at Verdun. The miracle of Verdun. The miracle of the Marne. The day of miracles is over for France.'

'And us?' Murray said. 'The English?'

'Ah, the English. Perhaps we're the miracle. For this time. For a time.'

'You said just now . . . blast villages out of memory. I don't see it. That might be the last refuge.'

'The last Verdun,' Ward said, smiling.

'No bomber can blast England out of memory.'

'Out of whose?' Ward said.

'Mine. Yours.'

'What can you remember?'

'A wall,' Murray said. 'It was curved back over the bank of a field higher than the road, the stones were covered with close moss like velvet, I peeled off damp cushions of moss with my fingers. A room in my grandmother's house when she lit the gas under a fluted yellow globe, she turned it up slowly, and the curtains were drawn over the bay window with the hyacinths. The coldness of the river in April in the sun. And one winter when I was at King's the fountain in the court froze, it was as though smoke had frozen, and I remember wanting to put my arms round it. Whatever happens—isn't that England?'

'Yes, as long as you live,' Ward said. 'Or as long as I live.'

Murray stood up and looked round the cellar. 'So it's only a question of seeing? And touching the fountain with the end of my finger? . . . I could feel its cold at the back of my brain. It was full moon, what they call clear as day, which is nonsense, there's nothing clear about moonlight. I went in then and drew the curtains in my room, and poured myself out the last half glass of sherry; I could turn in the room, turn on my heels, I could feel its warmth, I felt my body standing there. Very well, is that all? Where will it go afterwards, tell me that? Trees, the River Test, the downs, moss, fields, where are they to go?'

There was a sudden noise over their heads, the noise of men walking first on cobblestones in the yard, then on the wooden floor of the kitchen. Both men listened.

'Isn't there another memory?' Murray said.

## 5

Ward leaned forward and put the lamp out. They moved quietly in the darkness, the young man lightly and confidently, Ward with a dragging sound. The confused steps overhead went away into another room in the farmhouse. There was a moment's silence in the cellar before steps and voices returned overhead, and the hatch at the top of the stairs was pulled open. A torch flashed down, missing the Englishmen.

'A cellar, sir. Steps,' the German said.

He came down, slowly, torch held downwards in one hand, its circle of light slipping from step to step. He had his revolver in the other hand. He reached the bottom step and stood there, turning the torch towards the cellar on the right and raising it.

'Not difficult enough,' Ward said quietly.

The German swung round quickly and fired. Ward fired at the same instant, and the torch fell and went out. Three other Germans ran down the stairs. There were shouts and a scuffle in the darkness. The sounds were confused, there were no coherent voices, it was as though buried soldiers had begun to fight each other. The struggle lasted scarcely a minute. A fourth German, an officer, ran downstairs with a torch which he turned on one of his men huddled at the foot of the steps.

'Take him upstairs,' he said.

Two men half carried, half dragged the dead German up the stairs.

'Are you hurt?' the officer asked another of the men.

'In the arm, sir,' the man answered.

The officer turned away. 'Leave them until the morning,' he said curtly.

They went away upstairs and the hatch was dropped, like a plug, cutting off the feeble light from the kitchen. All the same, light, after an interval of a second or two, filtered into the cellar, and strengthened to a deceptive clarity, like the half-hour before dusk in summer when the sky closes in imperceptibly, so that apart from a sensation of failing sight it is still daylight, although reality is being sapped from the trees and hills on the horizon and the air presses like water on nearer objects.

6

The light showed a young officer in stained shabby khaki, standing, his back to the cellar, looking up the shaft to the yard. The shutters were open. Behind him, Major Ward had dropped asleep in his chair at the left of the table, his head on the Ancre or the Somme or some other of Redon's symbols. Richard Murray sprawled asleep on the floor. As he roused and got to his feet, the other young officer turned round.

'Hullo, you've taken your time to come up, I must say.'

'I got in the night before last,' Murray said slowly.

'Did you come through Mailly?'

'Couldn't tell you.'

'The way none of you people know your way about shocks me. I could walk from here to Albert with my eyes shut. I know every shell-hole and every stone, almost every smell. I very much doubt if the natives know their roads as well as the English army knows them.'

'Good,' Murray said. 'You're going to be useful.'

'Thanks.'

Murray frowned lightly. 'Is there any point in knowing them that thoroughly?'

'Ask no questions,' the other said, smiling, 'and you'll hear no lies. . . . Someone had the idea of sending us here for ever or the duration. Whichever rolls up first.'

'My God, I hadn't realised we were holding this place,' Murray said.

'In my humble opinion, it does the holding. I feel what you might call at home here. In a way I know it better than Burford, though I've lived there all my life.'

'Oh, I know it, there's an aerodrome,' Murray said.

'No. That's not the place.'

'In Gloucestershire.'

'There's no aerodrome,' the young officer said. 'You're thinking of some other Burford.'

'Probably.'

'It has one street, built down the side of the hill into the valley. A valley with deep greyish-

green sides, no different from any other Gloucestershire valley. The hills, if you call them hills, are
smooth, and there are stone roofs on the houses.
In winter—in summer, too, for that matter, but
the cold makes it more noticeable—you can hear
a cart on the road eight or nine miles off. . . .
When I go back I can recognise every sound, the
same branch creaks, the same magpies fly out
from the fir-tree at the same angle, the same
voices answer me in the shops. The only difference is that I don't take them for granted now,
and they hurt me.'

'You don't, in my opinion,' Murray said, 'see
any place until you've seen it from the air. I
thought I knew the Downs above Stockbridge,
I spend half my time riding on them when I'm
at home, I know all the paths. But the first time
I flew over them I could see which tracks have
been made by farmers and are only a few hundred
years old and which are the shadow of a road
made by Roman legionaries. Those roads reflect
upwards, you know. . . . You can see them from
an aeroplane. . . . And there are older marks still.
It's what I was saying, you can't drop England
out of memory.'

'Heard any peace talk?'

'What?' Murray said.

'Any idea of the war stopping, I mean.'

'Oh, that?' Murray said. 'If you ask me, it'll stop the minute the poor silly devils who started it realise there's nothing to be gained from going on.'

'As simple as that, is it?'

'I daresay.'

'I don't believe it. . . . Didn't you notice how things changed the minute war started? You were looking at the front of a house without thinking about it, it was ugly but peaceful and familiar. A minute later it pushed itself forward, insisting on being noticed, stupid, swaggering. That was because war had broken out in the interval. It's the same with anything you like. And it depends purely on an accident whether tonight or tomorrow you look at the sky and it turns its war or its peace face to you. A quite trivial accident. You never know what happened, what you did or forgot to do. All you know is you were free yesterday and this evening you're trapped. Yesterday you were depending on something, your job or a person you admire very much or the place you live in, and today you're all that stands between them and disgrace.'

'I daresay you're right,' Murray said. He yawned. 'I should like to go home.'

'Of course. . . . What were you thinking of when you said that?'

'A room with the curtains drawn across the window, a good fire for toast,' Murray said, 'red all the way up the bars. Quite an ugly room, the schoolroom, in fact, a long hard sofa, a large table, the rug in front of the fire has scorch marks. I always think of that room first.'

'The road down from the top of the hill to our house. My lightest steps, the ones I took when I was a child, left the heaviest marks, heavier than any I've made since, even carrying a rifle and my kit. I can never help walking in them.'

Murray walked over to the shaft and stood looking up. 'Extraordinary how far you can see from here. I can see the Ancre and a row of poplars.'

'If there were a hill of any sort in this part of the world you'd be able to see the Channel and Dover and Stockbridge and your favourite river.'

'I'll believe anything,' Murray said, 'of the air this morning. This country's not unlike my part of the world. The same hardness, you'd think it was indestructible.'

'You're wrong. Anything can be destroyed.

Except anything you and I remember. Any road I remember is safe, it can't change, if it did I should have forgotten it. . . . As I have been forgotten. . . .'

Murray yawned again, widely. 'I must go home.'

'Just as you like,' the other, smiling. 'They may not be expecting you.'

'See you again some time,' Murray said.

'S'long. Happy days.'

Murray went up the stairs out of sight. As he watched him go, the young officer had his back to the table. . . . Ward lifted his head, yawned, and stretched his arms. The young man turned round. Ward brought his hands down on the table, laughing, and jumped up.

'Jamie!' he said. 'What luck. When did you get back?'

*Oct.* 1940—*Feb.* 1941.